THE CLOSER

A BASEBALL LOVE STORY

ALAN MINDELL

THE CLOSER

For information about special discounts for bulk purchases, please contact Sunbury Press, Inc. Wholesale Dept. at (855) 338-8359 or orders@sunburypress.com.

To request one of our authors for speaking engagements or book signings, please contact Sunbury Press, Inc. Publicity Dept. at publicity@sunburypress.com.

FIRST SUNBURY PRESS EDITION
Printed in the United States of America
June 2013

Trade Paperback ISBN: 978-1-62006-240-1
Mobipocket format (Kindle) ISBN: 978-1- 62006-241-8
ePub format (Nook) ISBN: 978-1-62006-242-5

Published by:
Sunbury Press
Mechanicsburg, PA
www.sunburypress.com

Mechanicsburg, Pennsylvania   USA

ACKNOWLEDGMENTS

The author would like to thank the following for their wonderful help and support:

Bobbi Lona, Jerry Mindell, Paula Mindell, Devra Mindell, Jobi Mindell, Joe Mindell, Kea Warner and her San Diego area writers` workshop, Bonnie Owen, Nick Nichols, Linda Luke, Leslie Moffet, Judy Brown, Daisy Ramstetter, Heather Fritz, Daniel Levy, Ed Alston, Debbie Hecht, Judy Bishop, Lisa Wolff, Lief Hendrickson, Bill Gifford, Jon Udell, Gary Dolgin, Leslie Perlis, Hope Weissman, Debbie Klein, Therese Tanalski, Ginny Burt, Michele Vinz, Marvin Zuckerman, Fred Close, Eva Close, Christine Candland, Barry Withers, Jan Maxted, Lawrence Knorr, Janice Rhayem, William Gohlke, Debbie Gohlke, and the San Diego Swingcats.

CHAPTER ONE

It was the fifth inning and Terry Landers sat on the left field bullpen bench. To his right, fellow relief pitcher Clyde Alberts was fanning himself with his glove. Terry had never recalled weather this warm on opening day. But then this was Texas.

Earlier in the game, he had glanced into the packed grandstand and observed quite a few spectators wearing fine clothing, despite the heat. Of course he knew their attire had nothing to do with the beginning of baseball season. No, today was Easter Sunday and undoubtedly many people had come directly to the stadium from church, without going home to change clothes.

Terry certainly didn't feel like celebrating the holiday. It was 1999, the year he would make the jump from Triple A to the big leagues—the year he would spend opening day in Philadelphia. At least that had been his plan. The fact he was still in the minors—where he'd been fifteen years now —facing another hot Texas summer, left him less than festive.

"Mister...will you sign my scorecard?"

Terry looked over his left shoulder and saw a girl standing on the other side of the short green wire fence separating spectators from players. She had light-colored hair, blue eyes, and wore a blue dress. Perhaps she was eight or nine. Over the years, literally thousands of children had asked for his autograph. But there was something about her that made her stand out.

"You sure you want *my* signature?" he replied dryly.

"It's not for me," she answered curtly. "It's for my brother."

She pointed toward a boy who looked bigger and older than she, seated in the grandstand nearby, with a woman and a very young girl. She handed him a team program and pen. Ordinarily, he didn't sign autographs during a game, a violation of team policy. But the game was now between innings, and in his current state of mind, rules seemed almost incidental.

"What's your name?" he asked.

"Karen...Karen Riley."

"And your brother?"

"Billy."

"That your little sister there?"

"Tammy," she replied, nodding.

He addressed the autograph to all three children and handed her back the program and pen. She thanked him before leaving. He took a quick peek into the grandstand and watched her give the program to her brother, who smiled.

Terry Landers stepped off the mound, toward second base, and removed his cap. Using the wrist of his pitching arm, the right one, he wiped perspiration from his forehead. Despite the passage of several more innings and the afternoon now growing late, the temperature hadn't diminished.

Terry returned to the pitching surface. It was the top of the ninth and he had entered the game two batters ago, at the start of the inning. His team, El Paso, Philadelphia's top minor league affiliate, led Wichita 7-4—what should have been an easy "save" opportunity.

Except the first Wichita batter had lined Terry's initial pitch into center field for a single. And the next batter had walked on a close 3-2 pitch— much too close to take. Most minor league umpires would have given Terry the call, if only to speed up the game and get them all out of the heat sooner. This umpire evidently wanted to impress his supervisors though, regardless of any discomfort he caused.

With runners now at first and second, nobody out, Terry's first pitch to the next hitter, a knuckleball, was directly over the right hand batters' box, sending the hitter sprawling to the ground. Ball one. After getting the sign for his next pitch from the catcher, Bottoms, Terry wheeled off the pitching rubber and bluffed the second base runner back to the bag. The following pitch, another knuckler, drifted far outside. Ball two.

Collum, the squat sixtyish pitching coach, emerged from the El Paso dugout and walked slowly toward the mound, his expression grim, as if he didn't believe in Terry. More likely, he didn't believe in the knuckleball, Terry's main pitch. Not like Rick Gonzalez, the previous pitching coach, who had taught it to Terry, replacing a declining fastball with a pitch that sunk, danced and darted. But Rick was gone—to the big leagues with another organization, Oakland—leaving Terry behind.

"Get that thing over," Collum declared disdainfully after joining Terry and catcher Bottoms at the mound.

"Had the last guy struck out," Terry countered.

"And you're 2 and 0 on this guy. Throw strikes. Even if you got to go with your fastball."

Terry shrugged as Collum returned to the dugout. Wasn't it obvious how his pitching coach felt? He hated the knuckleball—which made no sense to Terry. Not in the current era of baseball, with its notorious lack of good pitching. At the very least, because the knuckleball didn't put as much strain on the arm as, say, the slider or split finger, a knuckleballer could give his team "innings" by pitching farther into a game and more frequently than other members of the pitching staff. Longevity was another benefit. Hoyt Wilhelm, relying almost exclusively on a knuckler, was an effective closer into his late forties. And the Niekro brothers—didn't one of them win 300 games, pitch into his fifties and make the Hall of Fame?

Maybe Collum's negativity was over Terry becoming pretty much a one-pitch pitcher. Since his fastball had lost its zip, batters could look for his off-speed deliveries, rendering his curve and change up almost useless, leaving the knuckleball his only viable option.

Rick had taught Terry a certain type of knuckler, one they called "the diver" because it suddenly dove toward the ground. At its best, it would sink from above the strike zone to a spot below the knees. When batters did make contact, the standard result was a weak grounder. Unfortunately, during spring training in Florida the last few weeks, Terry hadn't been able to get the usual dip on the ball, no doubt accounting for the hitters' success against him and his not making the leap to the majors.

3

Before seeking the catcher's sign for his next pitch, Terry again stepped off the mound, this time toward third base. As he once more wiped his forehead, he couldn't help noticing several people in the grandstand fanning themselves, either with cap, scorecard or newspaper. He should have become accustomed to the Texas heat by now, having played here the last two seasons, but his tolerance had actually declined.

He moved back to the pitching rubber. Bottoms flashed the fastball sign, no doubt influenced by Collum's admonition. Terry rubbed his jersey with his glove, shaking him off. Bottoms flashed the same sign again and Terry rejected it, realizing he was also rejecting Collum. Finally, Bottoms relented, flashing the signal for knuckleball.

After checking the runners, Terry fired "the diver"—a perfect one, sinking to the batter's knees, over the outside corner. The batter swung, making contact. The result was ideal for Terry, a two hopper to the shortstop, Clauson, a perfect double play ball, except Clauson bobbled it and it rolled behind him. The bases were now loaded.

Terry glanced at Collum in the dugout. No reaction, not even a little perfunctory encouragement. Terry considered backing off the mound again, but didn't. Why prolong this agony?

The next batter, a lefty, came to the plate and Terry peered in for Bottoms's sign. Knuckleball. Terry fired "the diver" and the batter fouled it off. Terry wasted no time before his next delivery, another knuckler. Another foul. Two strikes and no balls. He purposely threw a pitch into the dirt, hoping the hitter would chase. He didn't.

Bottoms flashed the knuckleball sign again and Terry fired. A perfect darting "diver" catching the inside corner at the knees. The umpire lurched, as if about to thrust his right arm into the air, signaling strike three. But he apparently changed his mind. Ball two. Once more Terry glanced toward Collum. This time the pitching coach did react—he motioned a pitcher in the bullpen to warm up.

Bottoms signaled fastball. Terry shook him off. Bottoms repeated the sign. This time it was Terry who relented. Maybe Bottoms was right to try the fastball.

4

Especially if this umpire refused to give them a break on the knuckler.

Terry fired the fastball. Inside, off the plate. But not far enough inside. The batter swung and connected, hitting a towering fly to right field. The ball always carried well on hot days. This one carried over the right field fence. Grand slam home run, El Paso now trailed 8-7.

Collum came out of the dugout again. He motioned for the pitcher in the bullpen to replace Terry. Head bowed, Terry trudged off the mound.

"Cupid's here," a voice greeted Terry Landers following a knock at his bungalow door.

"Come in."

Rich Harkey did. He was the El Paso first baseman. At 6 feet 7 inches, 240 pounds, he barely fit through the door.

"Me and Bottoms got three girls over my place," he said. "One for me, one for Bottoms, one for you."

"Triple date," Terry commented blandly.

"Yeah. Something like that. 'Cept I don't think they want to go out."

Terry thought. After his performance earlier, he could certainly use some company this evening. And Harkey's track record was pretty good. He'd arranged things many times before, normally during road trips, and they usually worked out.

"Yours is a little older," Harkey noted.

That's all Terry needed to hear. So, at age thirty-three, he was about to be regarded as the old man on the team again. In fact last season, other players—teammates and opponents alike—had started calling him "Gramps."

"I'd better pass," he said.

Harkey presented only brief resistance. Terry watched his hulking frame disappear into the darkness. What a striking contrast to his own build. Harkey stood out any time he entered a room. While he, Terry—at five-eleven, 170 pounds, with plain brown hair and eyes—hardly made an impression.

Harkey, at age twenty-one, was considered a "can't miss" prospect, unlike Terry, who evidently had no future.

*****

About twenty minutes later, because his bungalow was still very warm from the hot weather, Terry opted for a walk. His regular path took him right by Harkey's place. He decided to stop in front so he could possibly get a glimpse of "the older woman." But when he recognized shortstop Clausen's raucous laugh, he headed back home. Obviously, he'd been replaced in Harkey's lineup for the night.

The faint sight of his bungalow in the dark brought a smile to his face. He'd had it for two years, minus the seven weeks of Florida spring training during which he had given it up. Fortunately, a few days ago he'd been able to get it back, which was about the only good thing that had happened lately.

Certainly he'd done well enough last year to warrant surrendering the bungalow for a place in Philadelphia when he made his planned leap to the big leagues for this season. A 5-4 record, with twenty-five saves. Earned run average under 3.00. Of course that was with Rick Gonzalez as his pitching coach, not Collum.

As he neared the door to the bungalow, his smile turned to a frown. What else did he have besides this place and the clothes on his back to show for fifteen years in professional baseball? Not much. Wasn't it time to face facts? His baseball career had been a failure and he was wasting his time staying with it any longer.

Fifteen years. How many tens of thousands of wind sprints had he run? Or times had he simulated covering first base on grounders hit to the right side of the infield? How many hundreds of second-rate hotels had he stayed in during road trips? Or bus miles had he racked up?

Fifteen years with the same organization, Philadelphia. His resume read like a Greyhound bus schedule—stints at Rapid City, Keokuk, Bend, Walla Walla, Natchez, Savannah, Boise and now El Paso. Shouldn't loyalty and persistence count for something? Unfortunately, he knew the answer.

Maybe he should feel some gratitude. At least he had a job. Thirty-three year old career minor leaguers weren't exactly hot commodities. If he weren't a pitcher, even a knuckleballer, no question he'd be forced to try and find some other line of work.

And what were his prospects outside, in the "real world?" Two years of community college didn't exactly qualify him for a career in medicine, law or rocket science. Over the years, feeling bad about not getting a four year college degree, he had read a lot—psychology, history, different cultures. But reading didn't mean much on the job market. Nor did his non-baseball experience—brief stints as a shoe salesman, delivery truck driver, retail clerk, and delinquent-account collector.

He opened the door and went inside the bungalow, which sat behind the owner's house and was bordered on one side by a long narrow driveway. Like the outside, the interior was brown. Even the sparse furniture in the four small rooms was mainly brown, perhaps to conceal age.

He walked over to the television in the living room. On top of it was a picture of his father, who had died a couple of years ago at the family home in rural Indiana, soon after the death of his, Terry's, mother. His father had always encouraged his baseball, making it clear he wanted his only child to be a major leaguer. Not a very original sentiment, but without question it was partly responsible for Terry staying around the game this long.

His father had always emphasized working hard, sticking to the task, never giving up. Yet good things never seemed to happen to him, Terry, like they did to others. For example, Rick Gonzalez, now a big league pitching coach in Oakland, leaving him here in El Paso to deal with someone like Collum.

He flipped on the television. A big league game came on. He quickly turned it off.

He'd had enough baseball for one day.

CHAPTER TWO

Tonight's disguise wasn't among Elston Murdoch's favorites. Driving his rental car through deteriorated Chicago neighborhoods, he wore shades, a wide-brimmed hat and frayed clothing. Fairly standard stuff, certainly fitting the area, but if someone looked close, his outfit might not conceal his identity. On these streets, though, someone wasn't likely to look close.

Murdoch preferred last night's disguise. Full beard, orange hairpiece, checkered vest. His Dennis Rodman look, he had chuckled to himself. Not that it had brought him luck, however.

Tonight he recognized many leftovers from last night's cast. Drug dealers, women in tight skirts, wandering alcoholics. Despite being big, strong and, like the majority around here, black, he still felt a little apprehensive. The fact he'd injured an ankle earlier that evening, trying to make a shoestring catch in left field, no doubt influenced his mood, which wasn't helped by the fact that his team, Oakland, had now lost nine of ten games to begin the season.

Two or three times during his drive, he considered returning to the hotel to ice his ankle. Especially since he hadn't stayed at the stadium after the game to get treatment. But until he'd covered enough territory, he knew he'd keep driving. There was plenty of time for his ankle tomorrow, before the game.

Eventually, a drizzle began. Then it rained harder. Other than an occasional homeless sprawled in a doorway or under an awning, the area emptied quickly. As the rain persisted, Murdoch realized his task was futile.

He made a U-turn and headed back to the hotel.

When certain specific criteria are met, a "save" is credited to a relief pitcher who protects his team's late inning lead. A "blown save" is charged to a relief pitcher who could have had a save, but relinquishes his team's late inning lead. "The closer" is the relief pitcher regularly assigned "save" opportunities.

Terry began the season as the El Paso closer. By the end of the second week, though, his blown saves exceeded his saves by three. Unless he soon reversed the trend, he knew he'd lose his job. So, when Collum brought him into a game in Albuquerque with a 10-7 lead at the beginning of the bottom of the ninth, he welcomed the chance.

The first batter dispelled any notion that this would be an easy save. He hit a high fly that, in the late-night light Albuquerque air, cleared the left field wall. The second batter followed suit with a ringing triple that one-hopped the right center field wall. Runner on third, no outs, tying run coming to the plate.

Terry stepped off the mound. He certainly didn't have hot weather to blame for his outing so far, not with a cold wind blowing from left field to right. He had to get the next batter out.

He almost did. His third pitch, a 1-1 knuckler, danced nicely out of the strike zone. The hitter, a right hander, swung and tapped a soft grounder down the first base line. It should have been an easy out, but the ball hit the bag and squirted past first baseman Harkey, into foul territory. Double, 10-9, tying run on second.

The next batter didn't hit the ball much harder. He placed it perfectly, though—a looper that found vacant turf between the right fielder and second baseman for a single. The tying run moved to third.

Disgruntled, Collum emerged from the third base dugout and motioned toward the left field bullpen. Clyde Alberts entered the game. Terry's night was over. The four batters he'd faced had hit for the cycle in reverse—a homer, triple, double and single. Perhaps the most dreadful performance of his entire career.

Alberts threw only two pitches. A pop fly and double play grounder ended the game. El Paso won 10-9.

But Alberts, not Terry, got credit for the save.

*****

9

Elston Murdoch entered Cleveland Stadium through the players' gate. On the way down the long corridor to the visitors' locker room, he stopped briefly at an open door, which looked out at the vacant field. So many memories here. He led the league in homers one season. Runs batted in champ during another. And in his ten years here, he'd captured two batting titles. But that was all in the past.

His path took him by the home clubhouse. Even after three years since the trade in 1996, it felt strange not to go inside. He still knew some of the players on the Cleveland team, whereas he rarely talked to anyone on Oakland, his current club.

He entered the visitors' locker room. He was early, over an hour before the other players were due, and he was the first to arrive. He hardly ever got to the park before the assigned time, but today he had to get treatment on his ankle, which he'd reinjured chasing a fly ball in the left field corner last night.

The boo birds had been out again. Like they always were when he came to Cleveland. Loud as ever. In fact, while he lay on the ground in left field as Edwards, the Oakland trainer, examined his ankle, they'd actually taunted him and thrown things in his direction. It would be very easy to get even with them tonight. All he had to do was sit out the game because of his injury. They couldn't very well boo him if they couldn't see him, could they?

Since Cleveland was still paying almost all his salary, they thought they had the right to boo him. At least that's what many of the caustic comments hurled his way implied. But then, being booed was nothing new. He was booed every game, everywhere, home and away. Maybe it bothered him a little that the booing was worse in Cleveland. Lots worse. Like a dark cloud hanging over what he'd accomplished here.

The only way Oakland would make the trade, in which they sent Cleveland several young players, would be if Cleveland continued paying most of his salary. Of course, as a veteran of ten years, all here, he could have voided the deal. But with his marriage disintegrating at the time, he welcomed a change. Even with Cleveland a perennial pennant contender, and Oakland a constant doormat.

Didn't he get a bum rap here? They gave him a huge long term contract, at ten million per year, then assumed he'd singlehandedly bring them a World Series title. As if the mere act of spending big money would guarantee a certain number of wins. Disregarding the notion that each game's outcome occurred on the field.

The media had relentlessly dug into his personal life, all the way back to the ghetto days of his youth, when he kept less than model company. And of course they scrutinized his marriage, making him the culprit for everything that happened.

After changing into a light sweatsuit, he entered the training area of the locker room. Edwards was already there, prepared to give him his treatment. The thought crossed his mind that he hadn't sat out a game in more than two years. He also knew that Edwards was skilled at his profession.

Edwards would get him ready to play tonight.

"Got lit up a few days ago," Terry told Rick Gonzalez from his bungalow phone the day after the road trip ended in Albuquerque.

"I noticed."

"How?"

"Believe it or not...your old coach is gettin' to be a computer whiz. Keep up on things that way."

"Wow."

"See where you haven't been doing so good all season," Rick said.

"Putting it mildly."

"Hang in there."

"I was wondering..." Terry spoke hesitantly. "Could I send you a tape? Maybe you can spot something."

Terry realized his request might be unreasonable. After all, Rick was now with another organization. He had every right to decline.

"Sure," Rick said. "We're in Detroit tomorrow night. Send it to the hotel."

Terry knew that once Rick studied the tape, he'd be able to help. He always had. After getting the name of the hotel, thanking him and ending the conversation, Terry felt better.

But not much.

CHAPTER THREE

"You're not the closer tonight," Collum informed Terry in the bullpen right before the game with Oklahoma City was to begin.

"Oh," Terry replied, much more disappointed than surprised. "Alberts?"

"No. New kid. Tearing up A ball. They want us to give him a look."

Terry didn't respond. Instead he just sat on the bench and looked straight ahead. A ball from outfielders warming up rolled next to him, but he didn't even bother to pick it up.

"You're long relief tonight," Collum instructed and headed for the dugout.

"Long relief," words that stuck in Terry's mind—the lowliest job on a pitching staff—not good enough to start a game, nor to be trusted with a late inning lead—mostly mop-up assignments, or when the starter gets knocked out early.

The game began. The first two Oklahoma City hitters reached base, on a walk and a single. Not that any of it registered with Terry, he was so deep in thought.

Wasn't it clear where things were headed? With the new closer arriving, they'd have to make a roster change. Send someone to a lower minor league classification or simply release them. Most likely that someone would be him. Long relief tonight, gone tomorrow.

Maybe he should just step aside. Retire from the game once and for all, instead of letting things linger. Take action himself rather than wait for them to deliver the final humiliating blow.

Was there any hope? Even if the new kid couldn't cut it here, or was so good they promoted him to the majors, wouldn't there always be some other new kid to challenge

him? Someone younger and more talented than he.
Someone they wanted to look at, who *had* a future.

No question the younger players were getting better.
And, enticed by the burgeoning salaries of the late 1990s,
there was a steady stream of them. Plus they were getting
better coaching, better conditioning and better weight
training than when he broke in in the mid-80s.

Oklahoma City ended up scoring two runs in the top of
the first, when the clean-up hitter doubled in both
runners. Harkey tied the game in the bottom half on a
two-run homer. But Terry paid little attention, because he
was growing more and more disconsolate. He actually had
to fight back the impulse to simply trot off the field in the
middle of the game, in effect submitting his resignation
right then and there.

"Mister, can I have another autograph?" a voice asked
from behind him.

There was also a tap on his shoulder. He turned and
saw Karen Riley. She was standing next to him, on the
other side of the short green wire fence, looking just as
appealing as during their initial encounter, on opening day.

"What happened to the first one?" he questioned her.

"My brother took it to school," she answered. "And lost
it."

"Well...I guess he'll just have to come over here and get
another one himself."

"Oh no, Mister...I don't think he will."

"Why not?"

"He's too shy," she said after hesitating briefly.

"Sorry," Terry shrugged, refusing to comply with her
request.

She stood there a moment, looking confused. She
glanced at her family, sitting in the same place as on the
other occasion, nearby in the grandstand. Then she
turned back to Terry, who merely shrugged again. She
emulated his gesture, but he saw a tinge of resentment in
her expression. When she walked away, he tried to pay
attention to the game. Oklahoma City had gone ahead
again, 3-2, on a solo home run.

Several minutes passed before he felt another tap on
the shoulder. She stood next to him again, but this time

her brother stood behind her. He was tall and slim for his age, perhaps ten, with blond hair and blue eyes.

"Hi," Terry greeted him.

The boy didn't respond and his expression was blank.

"Your name's Billy?" Terry asked.

No response, except for switching his weight repetitively from leg to leg.

"How did you know his name, mister?" Karen interjected.

"You told me the first time. Your name's Karen and your little sister is Tammy."

She nodded. As on opening day, he addressed his signature to all three children.

"Billy's a pitcher, too," she said. "Just like you."

"I hope he's not a pitcher just like me," Terry muttered, almost to himself, while handing her back the program and pen.

Neither child responded to his self-deprecation. He hesitated, mulling over what he was about to suggest. Team policy advised against players fraternizing with spectators. But, considering his current status with the team, what difference did it make?

"Would you like to work out with me?" he asked Billy.

The boy smiled—a painfully shy smile which Terry interpreted as a positive reply. He asked the boy if he'd like to attend tomorrow night's game. Another shy smile. Terry told them he'd leave four tickets at the main stadium entrance and suggested they meet right here, in the bullpen, just after admission gates opened. One more smile.

After Billy and Karen left him and returned to their seats, Terry wondered if he'd made a mistake. Not because of team policy. No, what if he was no longer with the team tomorrow night?

CHAPTER FOUR

As Elston Murdoch headed for the right hand batters' box, the boos drowned out the sound of the Cleveland public address announcer introducing him. The game was on the line. Top of the ninth, Oakland trailing 5-4, tying run at first, one out. A double would likely tie the game; a homer would put them ahead of his former team.

Before stepping into the box, Murdoch gazed at third base coach Livingston for a prospective sign. He hadn't gotten a hit all night, his best effort being a fly ball to deep center. His batting average had dipped below his weight, 215, but he wasn't concerned. He'd always been a slow starter. And of course, he'd been hampered by the ankle injury.

Because of it, he was the designated hitter tonight. Therefore not playing left field, which at least saved him having to listen to the relentless hecklers out there. Here in Cleveland he usually attracted more than a thousand of them who monopolized an area just beyond the fence, directly behind him.

He assumed his regular batting position—slight crouch, straightaway stance—and stared out at the Cleveland closer, Minton, a left hander. Minton fired the first pitch, a curve, low and inside. Ball one, nowhere near the strike zone.

Murdoch wasn't the only Oakland player in a slump. In fact, the team as a whole had continued its dismal play, dropping fifteen of its first eighteen games. He'd love to win tonight, especially against his old team. Especially here in Cleveland, with everyone booing him. Since Oakland was leaving town tonight, following the game, he'd have the last laugh.

He checked with Livingston again for a sign. Hit and run? No way, not with him batting. Not when a double would tie, a homer would put them ahead.

Minton fired again. Another curve, this one outside and in the dirt. Ball two. He'd have to come in soon, or put the lead run on. Maybe a fastball in the hitting zone. Something to send into orbit.

Minton delayed by stepping off the pitching rubber. Then he made a couple of lethargic throws to first, chasing the runner back. Finally he delivered to the plate. A fastball in the hitting zone, just as Murdoch anticipated. Tailing toward the outside part of the plate.

Murdoch saw the pitch perfectly. He swung, and promptly felt the sweet sensation of solid contact. That home run sensation. Except this time he'd been slightly ahead of the outside tailing fastball. He did hit it sharply, but the ball stayed low. A hard one hopper right to the shortstop. An easy game-ending double play. With his bad ankle, Murdoch didn't even run to first.

Walking slowly back to the dugout, he heard the raucous Cleveland fans celebrating their victory. Then he heard the boos again—boos that quickly became jeers and taunts as he finally reached the dugout.

"This boy's got talent," Terry said to himself after catching Billy Riley's first actual pitch, once the two of them had warmed up playing catch.

The youngster had terrific natural movement on a fastball with surprising velocity for a ten year old. Plus he was left handed. Something Terry immediately envied, left-handed pitchers being prized commodities in the majors.

The sounds of El Paso taking batting practice in the background alternated with the sounds of Terry continuing to catch Billy's pitches, far down the right field line in El Paso Stadium. Harkey and Bottoms came over to watch. Before leaving, they both expressed accord with Terry's appraisal of Billy's ability.

"Where's your little sister?" Terry asked Karen Riley, standing nearby, on the other side of the little wire fence.

"Tammy?" she replied. "She's with Mama. They dropped us off and went home to pack."

"Going away for the weekend?"

"Not just for the weekend," she answered.

17

But their dialogue was interrupted when one of Billy's pitches caromed off Terry's glove and rolled away. By the time he retrieved the ball, in the process enduring Harkey and Bottoms ribbing him for not being able to catch a ten-year-old's pitch, he'd forgotten about Karen's comment. Minutes later, with his left hand getting sore from catching Billy's pitches, he decided to end the workout. As he and Billy walked over to Karen, he noticed the boy looked sad.

"We can do this again if you'd like," Terry told him.

Billy didn't answer. In fact he hadn't said a single word since he and his sister arrived. It was Karen who now replied.

"No. We can't."

"Oh?" Terry said.

"We're moving to San Francisco."

"Oh?" Terry repeated.

"Our uncle," she said. "He lives there. He's a doctor."

Terry then duplicated Billy's reticence, and he was sure, his own sad expression matched the boy's.

Elston Murdoch had an awful night again. From Cleveland, Oakland had flown to Baltimore, where he'd gone 0 for 5, dropping his average below .200. The team lost 14-3, giving them by far the worst record in the majors. In fact, they were on pace to compile one of the worst records in baseball history.

His postgame activities were also unsuccessful. His disguise for a drive through some of Baltimore's most rundown neighborhoods consisted of raincoat and rain hat. Not terribly original, but ultimately useful when, like in Chicago about two weeks ago, rain began pelting down.

He returned to the hotel much earlier than usual.

CHAPTER FIVE

"I got your tape," Rick Gonzalez told Terry over the phone very late one night. "Didn't see anything we couldn't correct."

Terry didn't reply. Partly because he was startled to hear from Rick at 3:00 a.m. And partly because he was groggy from sleep.

"Thought we'd work on it in person."

"Oh?" Terry managed. "You coming down here?"

"No. You're coming up here."

Again, Terry didn't answer. The late hour certainly had something to do with it. But of greater consequence, he hadn't a clue what Rick was talking about. A player didn't just up and travel during the season to work with a former pitching coach now with another organization...Unless...

"You've been traded," Rick said, providing the missing link that was just entering Terry's mind. "You fly out later this morning."

"To your Triple A?" Terry mumbled.

"No. Here. To Oakland."

"To Oakland?"

"Right. Your flight's already booked."

"You mean I'm in the *show*?" Terry said, still groggy and not convinced the entire conversation was no more than a dream.

"Congratulations."

"I don't believe it," Terry exclaimed.

"Believe it," Rick replied. "But I've got to warn you. We've got a bad team here. And an awful bullpen."

"Sounds like I'd fit right in," Terry managed, chuckling.

"That'll change," Rick answered seriously. "I've got a theory. Prevailing winds here favor the knuckleball. Especially your kind."

In his elation, Terry barely accomplished writing down the flight information Rick then gave him. After hanging up, afraid he'd wake in the morning and find this actually was no more than a dream and that he wasn't really in the major leagues after all, he purposely stayed awake the rest of the night.

Rick Gonzalez stayed awake too. But his reason was much different than Terry's. Very simply, he was too keyed up to sleep. What he hadn't told Terry was that he, Rick, had been promoted to Oakland manager yesterday. After nearly thirty years in professional baseball, he had finally gotten a real break. Last season, stuck in the Philadelphia minor league system as pitching coach in El Paso, wondering if he'd had his last big league employment twenty years ago when his playing days ended. Then, this January, returning to "the show," as Oakland's pitching coach. Followed only four months later by yesterday's news that he had become a major league manager.

Not that, lying in his bed near dawn, he had any illusions about the job. Without question, he was the beneficiary of simple economics. With the team playing so miserably, club administration was motivated to, in effect, abandon all hope for a successful season by aggressively cutting costs. Something they began with him. His salary would be nowhere near that of Lance Staley, the veteran manager he replaced. And they had already informed him they wouldn't be hiring a new pitching coach, that he would continue performing that function as well. In addition, they had fired the bench coach and bullpen coach. So, where other teams had a manager plus five or six or seven coaches, Oakland now had only Rick and two others, Clayton, a hitting coach, and Livingston, a fielding specialist.

Administration didn't stop there. Another way to achieve economy was to trade talented, albeit high salaried, players for players with some potential, but whose current earnings were low. The trade for Terry, completed just hours ago, was a perfect example. Oakland sent Jack Mott, an overpaid infielder in his option year, and Lonnie Frish, an often-injured outfielder, to Philadelphia in exchange for Myong Lee Kwan, a twenty-two-year-old Double A pitching prospect, and Terry, neither of whom would earn more than the major league minimum. Thus, Elston Murdoch's was Oakland's sole remaining big contract. No doubt they'd seek to trade him too, except Cleveland was paying virtually his entire salary.

Continuing to lay there, Rick knew, despite the negatives, he needed to remain positive. Actually, he didn't have much choice. He had a living to make, expenses to meet. He promised his wife before she died five years ago that he'd make sure their two daughters, both living in the family home in San Diego, and now in grad school, finished their educations.

It wasn't really his fault he'd never made good money in baseball. As a player, he'd come along too soon, well before salaries had mushroomed any place near where they were today. He was a terrific pitcher, known for his curve ball. Arm problems, however, shortened his career. Since, he'd been able to secure coaching positions, but climbing the minor league ladder had been slow and not especially rewarding.

At the first sign of daybreak, he got out of bed. The lack of sleep definitely hadn't helped his nerves. He knew he needed to do something today to pass the time. Maybe he'd meet Terry at the airport later on.

That would still give him most of the afternoon to prepare for tonight's game, his first as a major league manager.

"I feel honored," Terry said in the crowded baggage area of the Oakland airport, after Rick had approached and shook his hand.

"Why?" Rick asked.

"Never had a manager meet my flight. Especially a big league manager."

"You heard..."

"On TV at the El Paso airport before I left. Why didn't you tell me on the phone?"

"Guess it hadn't sunk in."

Terry observed that Rick's stint in the majors hadn't in any manner altered his appearance—tall and slim, with dark refined Hispanic features. Once they claimed Terry's luggage, Rick drove him a short distance to a pleasant neighborhood with small quaint houses and wide, tree-lined streets. Terry was amazed at how cool the weather was, especially for early afternoon, and the fact he actually had use for a jacket. Rick drove into a parking lot beneath a large apartment complex.

"Where are we?" Terry asked.

"San Leandro...suburb of Oakland...not far from the stadium."

"No, I mean this place."

"I live here," Rick replied while parking the car. "So do lot of the other guys. They let us rent short term for the season."

Terry nodded. He and Rick took his luggage to Rick's apartment. Then Rick gave him a full tour of the complex. Lavish landscaping, two swimming pools, Jacuzzis, gymnasium, tennis courts. Model apartments furnished exquisitely, complete with large television, stereo, VCR and housewares. All the amenities one could want.

"Definitely big league, "Terry remarked as they left the model.

"Checked this morning," Rick informed him. "Couple one-bedroom vacancies. You could move in now if you like."

"Seems a little rich...I better look around."

"Suit yourself. Till you decide, you can bunk with me. I got a pullout couch."

"I feel honored again," Terry chuckled. "Sleeping with the manager."

"Not with the manager," Rick quickly corrected. "In the manager's apartment."

Finally convinced Rick's phone call in the middle of the night wasn't a dream, Terry had permitted himself a brief nap on the plane to Oakland. He took another in Rick's apartment. Later that afternoon, while Rick reviewed some scouting reports and Oakland team statistics, he went out for a walk to familiarize himself with the locale. He'd never been in this area before. In fact, other than a brief stop at the Los Angeles airport, this was his first time in California.

He quickly noticed the small town atmosphere near Rick's apartment. Quaint library, several homey restaurants, plus numerous little stores and markets. If he settled here, he might avoid buying a car, like in El Paso. That is, if he could get a ride to and from the stadium. While walking, he even checked some bus routes, and found one went right there.

Heading back to Rick's place, within a block of it, he saw a "for rent" sign in the front yard outside a large house. The sign read "furnished bungalow," with an arrow pointing behind the house, along a narrow driveway. He was amazed that the setup looked almost identical to his place in Texas. And upon closer inspection, so did the bungalow itself—the outside was old and brown. He wondered if the inside was brown too, and the furniture also, to conceal its age.

He went to the front house. A thin elderly man answered his knock and led him back to the bungalow. And yes, other than having no air conditioning ("Don't need it here," the man explained), the interior was virtually the same. Almost as if, along with himself and his luggage, Terry had flown the bungalow in Texas to Oakland.

"How much?" he asked the man as they stood inside.

"Seven hundred a month."

"I'm a ballplayer. No telling how long I'll be here."

"Seven hundred a month," the man repeated. "For whatever time you're here."

Terry thought. How lucky to find this place, on his very first afternoon. But then there was Rick's apartment complex to consider. It certainly would be nice to live there. Regardless of the cost. After all, wasn't he in the big leagues now? And yet, who knew how long he'd remain? The way he'd pitched lately, it might not be more than a week or two. Regardless of his association with Rick.

"I'll take it," he told the man.

Terry's feelings of elation certainly didn't subside once he rode to Oakland Stadium with Rick. As they neared the parking lot entrance, he was absolutely thrilled by his first glimpse of the edifice. It looked colossal, bigger than any stadium he'd ever seen. And he loved its outline in green and gold, Oakland team colors.

Once inside, they walked to the team locker room, where he was further thrilled at the sight of his white uniform shaded in green and gold, with Number 20 and Landers stitched on its jersey back. Twenty minutes later, after donning the uniform, he was again thrilled when he stepped onto the splendidly manicured field for the first time, for pregame drills, and gazed up at the tens of thousands of seats surrounding him. And then meeting with Rick, the catchers and other pitchers as they reviewed scouting reports on that night's opposition batters, from Texas.

Texas. The mere mention of that name and his euphoric state of mind began to unravel. He started to feel tense, his stomach knotting, at the irony that this was their opponent in his very first game. Even with all the distance he'd traveled this morning from El Paso, he couldn't get away from Texas. He quickly questioned his choice of living quarters. Maybe instead of the bungalow, he should have selected something entirely different, something in no way related to his time in Texas.

But those were his thoughts before the evening really got bad—before Ronnie Laker, the Oakland starting pitcher, was knocked out of the game in the third inning—before Laker's replacement, Chaz Stewart, got shelled too—before Terry found himself on the mound at the start of the top of the fifth inning.

The score was already 12-1, Texas of course leading, when Terry fired his first pitch. It was a knuckler so far outside and in the dirt that it bounced past catcher Chris Bailey, all the way to the backstop. Once the umpire tossed him a new ball, Terry turned toward the outfield and took repetitive deep breaths. Considering that the afternoon had been cool, the evening inside the stadium was surprisingly warm, certainly no excuse for the chill he was feeling. Maybe he was simply in a state of shock.

He fired another knuckler. This one headed straight for the batter, in the right-hand box. Fortunately, the pitch

was so slow that he could easily duck out of the way,
which didn't keep him from glaring out at Terry.

"Better throw a strike," he muttered to himself after
more repetitive deep breaths. He did. Another knuckler.
Over the middle of the plate. The batter swung and
connected. Terry didn't need to turn around and look, the
sound of the bat told him where the ball was headed. He
finally did look, and saw that left fielder Elston Murdoch
hadn't even moved. A spectator at the very top of the left
field pavilion caught himself a souvenir.

"Great," Terry mumbled. "First batter in the bigs. A
tape measure job."

Things didn't get much better. The next batter singled
to center. Followed by a ground-rule double that bounced
over the right center field wall. Runners at second and
third, with no outs.

At least Terry was feeling warmer. He glanced at Rick
in the dugout. Rick's expression showed no emotion at all,
however. Almost as if he too was in a state of shock.

Terry pounded his fist into his glove with
determination. The next hitter was a left hander. No sense
considering intentionally walking him to load the bases
and set up a possible double play, though. Not with no
outs and the score already 13-1.

Terry threw a fastball. He got the grounder he might
have been looking for were the bases loaded. Except the
ball scooted past diving second baseman Collie Quinn.
Both runners scored and the batter went to second on a
play at the plate which wasn't even close.

Terry turned toward the outfield again and saw there
was action in the Oakland bullpen. So far, he definitely
hadn't been any better in the majors than he'd been lately
in El Paso. Again, he glanced at Rick—still expressionless.
Terry briefly scanned the grandstand and observed that
many people seemed to be leaving. Who could blame
them, with the score now 15-1?

He sized up the next Texas hitter, a tall skinny right
hander who wore his batting helmet to one side. Terry
decided to try a curve, a pitch he used infrequently. With
an open base at first, he didn't intend to throw it for a
strike. But it broke nicely, right across the plate. The

batter swung and lofted a long fly down the left field line. The ball kissed the foul pole for another home run.

Rick didn't even bother to come to the mound himself to remove Terry from the game. Instead he sent one of his coaches. While trudging to the dugout, Terry could only shake his head. What a debut in "the show." He'd given up five runs without retiring even a single batter. Earned run average of infinity. And likely a one-way ticket back to Triple A, or worse. Or, more likely, an outright release.

For the rest of the game and the remainder of the evening, Terry did manage to avoid Rick, so at least he didn't have to right away face the man who'd brought him to the majors. The man who'd done so much for him and his career.

After the game, he got a ride back to his bungalow with Collie Quinn, who lived in Rick's complex, a block away. And he was certainly relieved that, rather than having to spend the night at Rick's, he'd decided to rent the new place. Regardless of the fact that he associated it with Texas.

Very late that night, though, lying in bed at the bungalow, he couldn't help thinking about Rick. About how he had just endured an embarrassing 19-2 loss in his own debut, as a major league manager.

"Two things wrong with your knuckler," Rick told Terry. "One is, you've got to come more over the top. Your release point is too much from the side."

Terry nodded. Both wearing Oakland practice gear, they stood together in the right field bullpen at the majestic new ball park in downtown Seattle. Of course Terry had never been here, and he found his initial contact with the stadium breathtaking.

"And two," Rick continued, "you've got to keep your wrist stiff. I noticed you were bending it before you released the ball. That's fine for your fastball, not for your knuckler."

"I understand." Terry replied.

"The movement on your ball is too flat. We want more downward trajectory. Otherwise it's not a 'diver'. Didn't Collum point that out?"

"Collum hardly pointed anything out. We hardly spoke."

"Let me guess," Rick said. "Didn't like the knuckler."

Terry nodded again.

"Whole organization's pretty conservative," Rick commented. "One reason I didn't mind leaving."

Terry nodded once more. Their dialogue had been punctuated by sounds from a nearby batting cage, as Oakland players took turns hitting automated pitches. There was no game today and Rick had scheduled a voluntary practice. Tomorrow night's game would be the opener of a brief road stretch. Two days had passed since Terry's and Rick's ignominious debuts. They had lost again to Texas yesterday, but much more respectably, 5-2.

As he'd spoken, Rick demonstrated proper arm angle plus a stiff wrist, and, while holding a ball, showed Terry how it should move. This wasn't the first time Rick had presented these concepts to him and it wasn't difficult for Terry to understand.

During past sessions they'd had last year and the year before, Rick had offered other theories on the knuckleball, some of which were more difficult to understand. Things like digging fingernails into the ball at specific places, establishing a complete lack of spin or rotation on the ball, the role of a baseball's stitches in creating turbulence in the airflow, and even a brief lesson in aerodynamics.

"Normally, I take pitchers out of games myself," Rick said in an apologetic tone. "But I felt guilty the other night about you."

Terry looked at him questioningly.

"Throwing you to the wolves like that," Rick continued. "Right off the plane, before we had a chance to go over your delivery. But, I had a good reason."

Terry maintained his questioning gaze.

"I wanted to get a firsthand look myself," Rick explained, "at exactly what your problems were."

A slight smile crossed Terry's face. Here he was, in the big leagues. But more importantly, he was back with Rick.

CHAPTER SIX

Terry sat by himself on the bench in the right field bullpen. The same area of Seattle Stadium where yesterday Rick had given him instruction. He wasn't alone by choice. No, every other relief pitcher, plus one starter, had warmed up and entered the game already. And he'd become aware that the two catchers assigned to the bullpen, sitting in folding chairs almost 100 feet from him, preferred only each other's company.

It was the bottom of the sixteenth inning of what had been a very tense game. Oakland had gone ahead of Seattle 7-6 in the top of the sixteenth on a home run by Elston Murdoch, now almost fully recovered from his ankle injury. Carlton Denny, the Oakland closer, had just entered the game. Three more outs, Terry thought, and Rick would have his initial managerial victory.

Denny, a big right hander, fired his first pitch. The Seattle batter lifted a long fly to right, into the cold late-night air. Todd Slater, the right fielder, ran back to the wall. He leaped, but the ball hit the wall just above him, then caromed off his glove and rolled toward the foul line. By the time he retrieved it and threw it into the infield, the batter stood on third.

The infielders moved in for a play at the plate as the next batter, a pinch hitter for Seattle's weak-hitting second baseman, entered the batters' box. Denny, pitching carefully, walked him. The next hitter, the lead off man, also worked him for a walk. Bases loaded, tying run at third, winning run on second, with no outs. Terry grimaced. Rick might have to wait for his maiden win.

Denny began flexing his right arm and shoulder. Rick and Edwards, the trainer, trotted from the dugout to the mound. They talked with Denny before Rick turned to the plate umpire, who also came to the mound. Denny threw a practice pitch. Even from his vantage point some 200 feet

28

away, Terry could tell from Denny's body language that it hurt him. He continued to flex his arm and shoulder, then, accompanied by Edwards, headed to the dugout.

Rick pointed to the bullpen. Which, by simple elimination, Terry knew could mean only one thing. He was in the game.

"Go get 'em, Rook," one of the catchers shouted, confirming Terry's conclusion.

He took off the jacket he was wearing and trotted toward the mound. He immediately felt cold, could feel himself begin to shiver. The memory of those hot Texas nights, instead of this penetrating Seattle chill, suddenly didn't seem so bad.

"Sorry," Rick greeted, handing him the ball. "Looks like I'm throwing you to the wolves again. But I got no choice."

Terry's only response was to continue shivering. Rick remained nearby to watch him take his practice pitches. Because Terry was replacing an injured pitcher, he was entitled to as many as he needed. Not that the number mattered, since he sensed tonight he'd never really get warm. His first toss must have bounced a full ten feet in front of home plate, bringing a glare from the catcher, Chris Bailey.

The Seattle fans reacted too, promptly vilifying Terry's effort. Even with midnight fast approaching, the stadium was still full. Evidently the spectators anticipated their patience being rewarded, that with only a one-run deficit, the bases loaded, no outs and a rookie pitching, they'd soon claim victory. While Terry continued his warm-ups, the noise level radically increased, as if everyone present was going for the kill.

In all his years in baseball, he had never heard a crowd this loud. And here he was, the focus of their wrath. At a certain point, despite not actually feeling ready, either in body or pitching arm, he realized it was futile to continue the practice pitches. He'd never get any warmer. Besides, why prolong this agony? He motioned to the umpire and to Rick that he was set. Bailey came to the mound from behind the plate to review pitch signs.

"Good luck," Rick said, and he and Bailey left, Rick to the dugout and Bailey back behind the plate.

Terry heard a nearby train whistle, probably signifying an arrival at the station he'd learned was close. He glanced toward the outfield and observed fog beginning to descend on the stadium, giving the entire scene a surreal appearance. He felt almost as if he were a spectator to the drama unfolding, not the main character. Perhaps this was simply his way of dealing with his own anxiety, his only means of coping.

The numbers two, three and four men were coming to bat, the three best in the Seattle lineup. Terry noticed all the infielders playing back, willing to trade a run for a double play. Evidently, Rick would be satisfied giving up the tying run if he could force the game into additional extra innings.

The first batter stepped into the left hand batters' box and Terry looked at Bailey for the sign. Knuckleball. While going to the stretch position to hold the runners close to their bases, he reminded himself to throw "the diver" over the top, not the side, as Rick had instructed. And to make sure to keep his wrist stiff. He fired, and the pitch felt good leaving his hand, like it would get nice downward movement. The batter swung and hit the ball on one hop right back to Terry. He fielded it and quickly threw to Bailey, who touched home plate with his right foot and fired to first base. Double play, without the tying run scoring. Now there were two outs, runners on second and third.

Rick quickly trotted toward the mound. Terry wondered what he could want, and glanced instinctively at the bullpen. No one was warming up to possibly replace him. Then he remembered—there was no one left to warm up.

"Nice start," Rick said, matter-of-factly.

Terry admired his calmness. Bottom of the sixteenth, game on the line, more than forty thousand fans screaming, and Rick was his normal self.

"Pick your poison," Rick stated.

Terry looked at him blankly, clueless as to his intent.

"Gates or Casey?" Rick continued. "With the open base we don't have to face them both."

Terry gazed at the two hitters standing in the on deck circle. Gates, the left hander, perennial home run champ. Casey, right handed, currently leading the league in hitting.

"I'd walk Gates," Rick suggested. "Pitch to Casey 'cause he's right handed. Least they can't accuse us not playing percentages."

Terry nodded, muttering something almost incoherent about never being very good at mathematics. Then he was standing alone again, after getting pats on the rear from Rick and from Bailey, who had joined them on the mound. As he intentionally walked Gates, loading the bases once more, the crowd, seemingly louder than ever, booed.

Casey stepped to the plate. Terry heard another train whistle and gazed toward the outfield again, at the fog which seemed a little thicker. Was all this really happening?

He turned back toward Bailey, who flashed the sign. Knuckleball. Terry fired. Ball one, low and outside. Another sign. Another knuckler, this one catching the inside corner at the knees, for a strike. Casey lifted the next pitch foul, into the stands behind first. Then Terry threw one too far inside.

Before the 2-2 delivery, the runner at third danced off base, attempting to distract Terry. But Terry's concentration was good and he fired toward the plate. A perfect pitch, diving into the strike zone on the outside corner at the knees. The umpire flinched, as though about to raise his right arm, the "strike" sign. He hesitated, however, then signaled ball three. Bailey kept his glove positioned exactly where he'd caught the ball, right above the outside corner of the plate. Terry could only shake his head. But then, as a rookie, he knew better than to expect a called third strike in this situation, against the league's leading hitter.

He looked out at the fog once more, then up into the crowd behind home plate, most of whom were standing and yelling frantically. Here he was, in a spot he had always dreamed of as a kid—bases loaded, two outs, 3-2 count, and the game on the line—facing the league's leading batter. Was this really a dream? Or, more accurately, a nightmare?

He knew he had to come in to Casey, he couldn't walk him, walk in the tying run. He threw another "diver", a nice one, which Casey popped foul, off third. The third baseman, Jack O'Rourke, drifted to the grandstand railing and tried to reach beyond to catch the ball. But a spectator hit his glove and the ball bounced off, landing in the lap of a youngster sitting in the second row.

When Casey fouled away the next two pitches, Terry wondered how long this agony would continue. Did he have the nerve to keep throwing strikes to this dangerous hitter? Could he keep throwing strikes?

His next pitch *was* in the strike zone. Right in the middle of it. Casey swung and Terry knew by the loud crack of the bat it was trouble. The ball headed for deep left. He could see its flight briefly, and then lost it in the fog. Had Casey hit a home run? A grand slam home run, resulting in one more failure for Terry?

He *was* able to see Elston Murdoch, the left fielder, racing back to the wall. At the wall, Murdoch leaped, his glove high in the air, above the wall. For an agonizing moment Terry couldn't tell whether the ball landed in Murdoch's glove or on the other side of the wall. Then he saw the second base umpire, who had run into the outfield, thrust his right arm into the air, signaling "out."

The game was over. Oakland had won.

Frequent joyful shouts pierced the Oakland locker room, players proclaiming their victory. Several came over to Terry and offered congratulatory handshakes and backslaps. All the attention of course felt great. So did the locker room's warmth, welcome relief from the late-night Seattle chill.

Terry's first priority, even before showering, was to approach Elston Murdoch and thank him for the terrific catch. Several media persons surrounded Murdoch though, despite his repeatedly shaking his head, obviously refusing to talk. When they dispersed, Terry went over.

Once he got close, he was astounded by how large and powerful Murdoch looked. He must have been at least 6 feet 3 inches, 220 pounds. Black body naked except for the trousers of his uniform, he had the hugest chest, shoulders and forearms Terry had ever seen on a baseball player. In fact, Murdoch resembled more the football prototype—a fullback or a linebacker—than a skillful outfielder.

His head seemed too small, no doubt because of his massive physique. His face was handsome, in a rugged way. But he had an unhappy expression, especially for someone who had just been so prominent in his team's victory.

"Thanks," Terry greeted, extending his right hand.

Using a simple gesture of his own right hand, however, Murdoch waved him away. Then he turned toward his locker, grabbed a shirt and hastily began putting it on. Nothing for Terry to do except return to his own locker. Once there, he did glance at Murdoch a couple of times, noticing that he continued to dress rapidly, straight from his uniform to street clothes without a shower, as if eager to be somewhere quickly.

"At least it's not just us he won't talk to."

Terry turned to see a fortyish man gazing at him, wearing a worn business suit. Terry looked at him mutely several seconds before realizing he was probably a member of the media.

"Mind if I ask you about your first save?" the man continued. "As a major league pitcher."

"Rather you ask Rick Gonzalez," Terry replied uncomfortably. "About his first win as a major league manager."

Throughout the Seattle series, Terry watched Rick closely. He found him no different as Oakland manager than pitching coach in Texas—so unlike other managers and coaches he had played for, who were critical, gruff, distant, and aloof—always a barrier between them and the players, which no one dared cross.

No question the players liked Rick. Everyone, that is, except Elston Murdoch, who evidently liked no one, which didn't seem to bother Rick. He simply wrote Murdoch's name in the third spot of the lineup card every day, and left him alone. Terry never saw them converse or communicate in any other way.

The players played hard for Rick. Apparently no one minded getting their uniform dirty. Diving for a ball in the outfield. Digging for the extra base. Sliding hard to break up a double play.

All the above occurred during the next two games in Seattle, both wins, giving them a series sweep before they returned home to Oakland.

CHAPTER SEVEN

"Mister...can my brother play with you again?"

By the sound of her voice, Terry knew who it was right away. Yet, lying on the grass near the left field bullpen, doing stretching exercises, he still did a double take. Yes, definitely, it was Karen Riley, wearing the same cute little blue dress she wore at their very first meeting, back in El Paso.

"What're you doing here?" he managed, still on the ground.

"We came to see you play," she replied, as if her answer were apparent.

He got up and moved closer to where she stood, just above him in the grandstand, in an aisle next to the first row of seats. As he looked up at her, the late-afternoon sun was shining directly in his face and he had to take off his cap and use it to shield his eyes.

Since that evening's game was still nearly two hours away, very few spectators were present. In fact the crowd was so thin he easily spotted Billy Riley about ten rows above, wearing his glove.

"How'd you know I was here?" he asked her.

"My brother...he found out. He listens to all the games on the radio."

"He knows my name?"

"I think he knows all the players' names."

Terry, except for a smile, didn't respond. He was still startled over the fact she and her brother were actually here.

"Well, Mister," she said a little impatiently, "you going to let him play with you like last time?"

"Is your mother here?" he asked after slight hesitation.

"Yes. With my sister."

She pointed about halfway up the grandstand, perhaps twenty rows, to the same woman Terry had seen at the game in El Paso. Little Tammy sat directly in front of her.

"I need to speak to her," he said

After giving him a less than cordial look, Karen climbed the stairs to her mother, providing him a minute or so to think. This wasn't the minor leagues, where teams might not be so rigid about spectators entering the field. Where he really wasn't so concerned if they were rigid. No, this was the majors, where things were going well, and he didn't want to risk breaking any rules.

As he waited, several youngsters neared, seeking autographs. An hour or two before the game, while players warmed up or practiced, was always the best time for that. Hoping not to keep Karen's mother waiting, he reached over the grandstand railing for pencils, pens, programs and scorecards being thrust at him, and quickly obliged.

Once the youngsters left, he saw her standing alone in almost the exact spot her daughter had just vacated. He moved to her other side, to where he didn't have to squint into the sun to see her. She had light-colored hair and unusual sparkling hazel eyes. Though thin, her face was pretty. Her figure also seemed thin, beneath simple slacks and blouse, and a green jacket.

"Thanks for coming to the game, Mrs. Riley," he said.

"I really have no choice," she smiled. "Since your workout with Billy, that's all he ever talks about. He was thrilled about your trade."

"I'm surprised he heard about it."

"When it comes to baseball, my son doesn't miss much. Wish he paid as much attention to other things..."

Terry grinned. Then he glanced at Billy, still sitting some ten rows away. He'd love to work out with the boy, right here, right now. But there was no way.

"I'm afraid there's a problem," he said. "It's against league rules to invite him on the field."

"I understand, Mr. Landers."

"Terry," he said, flattered that, like her son, she knew his last name.

"Lauren," she replied.

36

There was a pause, and he looked back up at Billy. Then back to Lauren Riley. He couldn't tell her age. About his, he guessed.

"I'm sorry you made a wasted trip," he said

"It's not wasted," she smiled. "We came to see you play."

"I'll make you a promise," he answered. "If you'll give me your phone number and address, first open day I'll come over and work out with Billy."

She complied and wrote out the information on a piece of paper and handed it to him. After she left him, he watched her go to Billy, put an arm around him and walk with him to where Karen and Tammy sat.

His attention was then diverted by a new bunch of kids approaching, seeking autographs.

The Rileys weren't Terry's only surprise that evening. Just before game time, Rick came to him in the bullpen and informed him he'd be the closer.

"For tonight?" Terry asked.

"For's long as you can do the job," Rick answered. "We just put Denny on the DL."

Rick explained that after two separate MRIs on Denny's arm and shoulder, specifically his rotator cuff, the team doctor had determined an operation was necessary. For now, they placed Denny on the 60-day disabled list, but undoubtedly he'd be inactive the rest of the season.

"So you're it," Rick declared. "I don't think any of the younger guys are ready for the pressure."

"You think I am?" Terry asked.

"You're not ready by now," Rick answered. "When will you be?"

Terry wasn't sure he liked Rick's reference to age. There was no questioning his logic, though.

The Rileys evidently brought Terry plenty of luck that night. Not only did Rick assign him the closer role, but he got another save, this one much easier than the one in Seattle. Though he did enter the game with the bases loaded in the top of the ninth against Kansas City, there were already two outs and he had a five run lead, 9-4.

Not that, like in Seattle, he didn't require some good fortune. The first batter hit a sharp liner to the gap in right center, which rolled all the way to the wall. But when the batter stumbled and fell rounding second, shortstop Felix Oates took the relay from the outfield and tagged him before he was able to scramble back to the bag.

The win was Oakland's fourth in succession.

Later on, well past midnight, Terry decided to leave his little bungalow for a walk because he couldn't fall asleep. So much had happened recently, and so quickly. In less than a week, he'd been traded, gone to Oakland from El Paso, gotten his first two major league saves, become reacquainted with the Rileys, and been named Oakland closer. After thirty-three years of very little happening in his life, all this was a bit unnerving.

It was another cool night, plainly one more thing to get accustomed to. As he began walking around his new neighborhood, a dog howled in the distance. Actually, it sounded like a wolf, reminding him of his days in the country, as a boy, growing up in Indiana.

He thought of his father. How nice it would have been if his dad were still alive to see him pitch that last inning in Seattle. Either in person or on television. How nice it would have been to send him the tape of the game. Possibly even watch it simultaneously, each on their own VCR, Terry in California, his dad in Indiana two thousand miles away, connected by telephone.

His father would have loved the idea Terry was now a big league closer. No matter how long it lasted. And Terry would have loved to tell him that after all these years, his advice—sticking to the task, not giving up—had finally paid off.

As he crossed a street at an intersection, his thoughts were interrupted by a commotion just ahead. Tires screeching, car doors slamming, loud angry voices. His initial instinct was to turn and head back to his place. No sense looking for trouble this late at night. But then he heard a thud, as if someone were being shoved against a car. And he was able to decipher the words of one of the angry voices.

38

"Hey, Mr. Ten Million, use some a that big money, buy a bodyguard...new disguises."

Because maybe something seemed familiar, Terry edged closer. He could barely make out two cars in the street, one parked at an angle in front of the other, as though it had cut it off. Then he saw someone large, surrounded by four men. Another thud ensued, and this time he was sure it was from the large man being shoved against a car, the one that had been cut off.

"Why you nosin' 'round our territory?" the same angry voice shouted.

Terry moved closer yet, within fifteen or twenty yards. Although he still couldn't see that well, he suddenly realized who the large man was. It was Elston Murdoch. No question, it was Elston Murdoch.

What should he do now? It certainly wasn't his quarrel. And yet Murdoch was his teammate. Murdoch had made the terrific catch for him in Seattle. And Murdoch was now in trouble, being attacked by four men.

Terry noticed that the other car, the one not being used to shove Murdoch against, was still running. He rushed to it and scrambled inside. He gunned the engine and, to the shouts of Murdoch's attackers, sped off.

In the rearview mirror, he saw the four men jump into the other car and begin to follow. It was the start of a high speed chase. Not exactly what he had in mind when he strolled out of his bungalow a little while ago.

Fortunately, the chase lasted no more than about thirty seconds. A police car, probably summoned to the scene because of all the commotion, entered an intersection just before he did, and he nearly broadsided it, swerving and stopping just in time. The police car also stopped.

Would the four men stop too? His question was quickly answered when they whizzed by, barely missing the police car themselves. He saw them turn left at an ensuing intersection and felt, at least momentarily, slightly relieved. Not that they couldn't easily turn around and come back.

He didn't know what to do next, so he did nothing except stay in the car. Two policemen got out of their vehicle and came toward him. Just then Murdoch, breathing heavily, clothing awry, trotted onto the scene.

"My car," he panted to the officers. "Been stolen."

"This car?" one of the officers asked him, pointing to the one Terry was in.

"No. Bunch of guys roughed me up. Drove off in it."

"He one of them?" the officer inquired, motioning toward Terry.

Murdoch shook his head.

"You know him?"

Murdoch nodded.

"Want to give us a description of your car?"

Murdoch nodded again.

While Terry remained in the car, Murdoch accompanied the officers to their vehicle. Terry watched as the three of them began processing a police report on Murdoch's car. He wondered whether the officers would want to question him too, once they finished with Murdoch. Minutes later, Murdoch came back alone. Terry saw that his clothing was still unkempt. And his expression grim.

"Take me home," he directed Terry, getting into the car.

"Sure."

After glancing quickly at the policemen, who remained in their vehicle, Terry started the engine and began to drive off.

"Sorry about your car," he said.

Murdoch didn't reply.

"Any chance the police will recover it?" Terry continued.

"No chance," Murdoch answered sullenly. "Those guys got it stripped by now."

"Then how come you went through all the trouble making a police report?"

"Smokescreen," Murdoch replied.

"Smokescreen?"

"Mine wasn't the only car stolen."

Terry could feel his facial muscles contort as he realized that, technically, he had committed a crime.

"What do we do with this one?" he asked anxiously.

"Park it where you found it," Murdoch answered. "Guarantee...those guys'll pick it up by morning."

"You know those guys?"

"Never seen them before in my life."

"Thanks for not implicating me," Terry said while parking the car in almost the exact spot he'd taken it from.

"Least I could do...way you saved my ass."

"Least I could do," Terry replied. "Way you saved *my* ass...that catch in Seattle."

Terry couldn't be certain in the dark, but he thought he detected a slight smile cross Murdoch's face.

The first thing Terry did after getting up early the next morning was return to where he parked the car with Murdoch last night. Murdoch was right. The car was gone.

CHAPTER EIGHT

Terry entered the game at the start of the ninth inning, with Oakland leading 3-2. He sensed this wouldn't be easy. He'd be facing Boston's four, five and six men in the lineup, all of whom had hit the ball hard earlier that evening.

One thing was to his advantage, though. There was a strong wind—the prevailing one Rick had alluded to the night he informed Terry of the trade, the wind he said would favor the knuckleball. It was blowing off the nearby bay in an easterly direction, from the third base dugout toward right field. As Terry warmed up on the mound, he could tell "the diver" had extra break to it, both down and away from a right hand batter.

The first hitter swung at the first pitch, topping a weak grounder to first baseman Phil Steiner. Terry raced toward first base, received Steiner's toss and stepped on the bag. One out. Two more and Oakland would record its eighth consecutive win, a streak that began with that initial victory in Seattle.

Yesterday's newspaper had featured a lengthy article on the team's resurgence. It gave most of the credit to the pitching staff, especially to the young starters like Myong Lee Kwan, who had come over with Terry in the trade. But Terry would argue that Rick was the major difference, working tirelessly in the bullpen, before and often long after games, tutoring pitchers on arm angle, release point, follow through; keeping baserunners close, developing new pitches.

The next batter took a called strike before bouncing weakly to Collie Quinn, halfway between first and second. Terry again headed for first, but stopped when Steiner, after starting for the ball, reversed himself and got to the bag to handle Quinn's throw. Two outs.

Yesterday's newspaper carried another story Terry read with interest, though with more concern. It disclosed the theft of Murdoch's car and that no progress toward recovery had been made. While there was no mention of him, Terry grew uneasy that the incident reaching print would heighten investigation and possibly lead to his eventual involvement.

He considered approaching Murdoch for an update. But when he had looked across the locker room at Murdoch at his locker after last night's game, he seemed, as usual, eager to leave. And, within seconds, was dressed and gone.

The next batter tapped the first pitch right back to Terry, who threw to Steiner. Three outs, all easy grounders. After only four pitches, Terry had his third save.

Maybe there *was* something to Rick's "prevailing wind" theory.

Terry's first direct contact with San Francisco occurred when he emerged from the subway station a few miles southwest of downtown. He was promptly greeted by a heavy fog, much thicker than the one in Seattle the night of his first save. If he'd found Oakland and San Leandro cool, even cold, San Francisco was freezing, especially for mid afternoon. An icy wind seemed to blow right through him. He soon experienced the hills the city was famous for, ascending and descending them as he walked to his destination, a small white house about a mile away.

Wasn't it time to buy a car? Subways, buses, and begging rides from teammates were growing tiresome. He now resided in an area with plenty to do and see. All he needed was a convenient means to get to them.

In El Paso, at least he had excuses. He could walk to the ball park. The few entertainment activities were close. And, unlike now, a car would have been a luxury he really couldn't afford.

No matter the logic, though, he knew he'd wait. Let at least two or three big league paychecks come in. After all, things could quickly change. Denny had gotten hurt, opening the door for him, Terry, to become the closer. It could just as easily be him on the disabled list. Or he could fall back into the slump he'd experienced in El Paso. A couple of weeks in the majors certainly didn't guarantee he'd stay.

Despite the fog, he found the small white house. He rang the front doorbell. Karen Riley opened the door, little Tammy standing right beside her. Billy, wearing a baseball glove, stood in the background of what Terry could see was the living room.

"Ready?" Terry asked.

"Mommy, can I go too?" Tammy asked Lauren, who had entered the room.

"No, sweetie, it's too cold. You stay here with me."

"Any suggestions where to go?" Terry asked Lauren, now at the door.

"There's a little park in the next block. Billy and Karen know the way."

"Mommy, I want to go too," Tammy squealed.

"No, honey. Maybe we'll walk over in a while."

Lauren was right about the park being close. Their only problem locating it was caused by the fog, now extending clear to the ground, which, together with the cold, no doubt accounted for Terry's inability to consistently catch Billy's pitches. Plus the fact that his left handed deliveries had so much movement, even more than Terry remembered from their previous workout, weeks ago in Texas. Fortunately, Karen was there to help him retrieve.

"Your brother has a terrific arm," Terry told her at one point, after she'd picked up the ball and handed it to him. "I guess he practices with your father."

"He used to," she answered. "Before my father died."

Terry felt bad. Not that this information should have been totally unexpected, since none of his previous encounters with the Rileys involved a paternal figure. What did surprise him, however, was her candor in presenting the news. Of course he hadn't had time to get a clear reading on her. All he knew for sure was that her assertiveness seemed to counteract her brother's shyness.

After Billy had pitched nearly half an hour, Terry called him over. He clarified the strike zone and offered some

44

pitching strategy. Then he explained how to do wind sprints. After the youngster had done several—repetitions of running full speed fifty yards and walking back to the starting point—their workout was over.

"One thing, Billy," Terry said as he, the boy and Karen left the park. "No curve balls."

Billy, though definitely listening, didn't reply.

"I threw too many when I was a kid," Terry continued. "Hurt my arm. Now I've got nothing left on my fastball."

The boy kept listening.

"No curves," Terry reemphasized. "But next time I'll teach you a change up."

While heading back to the house, they almost, quite literally, ran into Lauren and Tammy. The truth was, had their paths not converged, they might not have spotted them in the fog. Tammy wore a tiny green baseball cap, while her mother had on the same green coat she'd worn at the game.

"I think Billy's got a future in baseball," Terry told Lauren as all of them walked together.

"You can say that when he's only ten."

"I can say that *because* he's only ten. I wish I had his arm. Plus he's left handed."

Terry then presented the common baseball adage that left handers, especially pitchers, were at a premium. The demand for good ones far exceeded the supply. If Billy developed like Terry anticipated, many more doors would open to him than to right handers.

"Ever consider Little League?" he asked the boy.

"See. I told you," Karen chimed in.

"I could check with some of the guys," Terry said. "See who knows a good league."

The boy smiled.

While they continued walking, Terry considered asking about why Billy never spoke, at least in his, Terry's, presence. He also considered asking about the children's father. But then this might not be the time nor place, so he didn't. Instead, he noticed the little white house as they neared it, and observed that it seemed to glow in the fog.

"Do you own?" he asked Lauren at the front door.

"No," she answered promptly. "Come in and I'll make us all a warm drink."

"Afraid I can't. We leave on a road trip tonight and I still haven't packed."

Did she look disappointed? He couldn't tell. After unlocking the door, she thanked him for coming, extending her hand. When he took it, he noticed how small it seemed inside his. Heading off, he waved good bye to the children, who returned the gesture.

During his long walk back to the subway station, the wind was just as cold. But the fog appeared to dissipate.

CHAPTER NINE

"Hey, Black Boy...nice to see you again."

Once more, trotting to left field to begin the bottom of the ninth in Toronto Stadium, Elston Murdoch heard the same shrill male voice that had heckled him all night. Coming from just beyond the foul line in the first row, no more than fifty or sixty feet away from where he normally played on defense. Like the guy had measured the closest seat to him and that's the one he bought.

"Hey, Black Boy...only time I'm here is when *you* come to town."

"Man," Murdoch muttered to himself as he threw a warm-up toss to someone in the Oakland bullpen. "Can't he come up with something fresh?"

Evidently not. Every single comment all night long had been prefaced by "Hey, Black Boy." And, as his last statement inferred, he had ragged on him before. In fact, Murdoch remembered him from trips here several years ago, back in his days with Cleveland.

"Hey, Black Boy...looks like the hitting streak's over."

He was right. Murdoch had gotten at least one hit in fourteen consecutive games, a streak that began with the game-winning home run in Seattle. But tonight against Toronto, he was 0 for 4. The streak had ended, unless the game went into extra innings, which might actually happen, since it was now tied 4-4.

"Hey, Black Boy...after the game, gonna go beat your ex-wife?"

This guy never let up. During the course of the game, in addition to Murdoch's marital problems, he had introduced his legal difficulties, his years in Cleveland, even his childhood. Murdoch had to give him credit for at least one thing though—he'd certainly done his homework.

The truth was Murdoch did have an exchange with his ex-wife, except right before the game, not after as the heckler was suggesting. She had reached him by phone in the clubhouse. Their regular unpleasant dialogue about money. She had none left, as usual, and would he send more? She called at least three or four times a month, always managing to locate him, no matter what city he was in.

"Heard from Carly?" he had asked her, also a regular subject.

"No."

"Any idea where she is?"

"Your guess is as good as mine."

"Where was she when you heard from her last, Sheila?"

"Denver, I think...or maybe San Antonio."

"You're a terrific mother," he had said angrily.

"No worse than you were a father."

This was how their conversations usually ended. Then one of them would hang up on the other. Tonight it had been Murdoch doing the honors.

The marriage had probably been doomed from the start. Simply put, they were too young, the wedding occurring before either of them graduated from their inner city Philadelphia high school. But Sheila was already pregnant with Carly, and Murdoch, about to sign his first professional baseball contract, wanted her with him for his initial minor league assignment.

She had trouble adjusting as a baseball wife—staying home alone with their daughter while Murdoch went on road trips, moving frequently while he rapidly climbed the minor league ladder. And then there were the drugs. By the time he reached the majors, her recreational habit had become full blown. Plus, she'd taken to alcohol, which neither mixed well with the drugs, which had mushroomed into an arsenal, nor her personality.

Of course Murdoch was no bargain himself, his anger and bad temper often spoiling what little harmony they had. But he did keep fighting for the marriage, steadfastly postponing the inevitable. He had good reason though. Very simply, he adored his daughter.

Finally, about three years ago, when Carly was twelve, the divorce occurred. Things between Murdoch and Sheila had gotten so toxic by then that he paid off her alimony and child support entirely, in one huge lump sum, hoping not to have to deal with her again. Standing now in left field, he knew what a useless gesture that had been.

"Hey, Black Boy...Ever think about that guy you sent up the river?"

Murdoch felt himself grow angry. Not about this guy or his comments—he was a jerk. No, he was angry over the memory of the media being so diligent in ferreting out the sordid details of his life, then making public various implications and innuendos that had only the slightest grain of truth.

They could have let it go at his marriage, which was bad enough. Had they, he might have even agreed to talk to them again. But they had to keep digging and digging.

One of their stories was what this guy was referring to in his last comment. How he, Murdoch, had avoided prosecution and inevitable jail time for drug possession by paying someone to take the rap for him. The only shred of accuracy in their entire account was that he did know who took the rap.

The first Toronto batter in the bottom of the ninth, after fouling off several pitches, worked the count to 3 and 2. He lined the next pitch into right center for a double. The Toronto manager sent in a pinch runner for him. The next batter dropped a sacrifice bunt down the first base line, advancing the runner to third with only one out.

"Hey, Black Boy...party's almost over."

Murdoch tried to ignore the fact the guy was probably right. Along with the other outfielders and all the infielders, he moved way in, trying to keep the winning run from scoring. The next two Toronto batters were intentionally walked, loading the bases, creating a force play at home and potential double play. From the dugout, one of the Oakland coaches waved Murdoch even farther in, and over toward left center.

The next Toronto batter didn't cooperate with this alignment. He hit a fly near the left field line, close to the area Murdoch had just vacated. Murdoch raced over and made a one hand catch. Now the difficult part—trying to throw out the runner from third base, who had tagged up with the catch and began speeding to the plate. Murdoch planted his right foot as best he could on the Toronto Stadium artificial turf, then took a couple of quick hopping steps and hurriedly fired toward Bailey, the catcher.

Watching the ball descend, Murdoch knew his throw would have to be perfect to keep the game alive. Ball and runner arrived at their destination simultaneously, the runner sliding, but Bailey blocking the plate as he caught the ball. The umpire elevated his right arm. Extra innings.

"Hey, Black Boy...nice goin'. We get to party some more."

When Murdoch reached the dugout, several teammates came over, offering high fives. He motioned them away though. He was scheduled to bat fifth in the top of the tenth, but when the first two Oakland batters struck out, it appeared he'd have to wait until the next inning—if there were a next inning. A subsequent single and walk, however, brought him to the plate.

His arrival there was greeted by the usual loud boos, but not loud enough to drown out his companion along the left field line. Was he using some kind of amplification, or was his voice just naturally shrill?

"Hey, Black Boy...good thing you kept the party alive. Now you can make an out and go 0 for 5."

Murdoch had to smile to himself. Evidently, this guy was now into rhyme. As the two runners edged off their bases, Murdoch took a couple of practice swings. The bat felt great in his hands, like it had all the time lately. During the streak, he'd raised his average about sixty points. Not unusual for him this time of year. As the weather began to warm up in the East and Midwest near the end of May, so did he.

When he got hot like this, he didn't care who was pitching. Often he didn't even *know* who was pitching. First good pitch, rip away. Exactly as he did now.

It was a curve, outside corner at the knees. He didn't try to pull the pitch; instead, he went right with it. Heading to first, he watched the ball land in right center and roll all the way to the wall. Double, both runners scoring. Oakland led 6-4. Hitting streak now fifteen.

Trotting to left field for the bottom of the tenth, Murdoch actually looked forward to the shrill voice. Who got the last laugh, pal? But he attained no such satisfaction. He even looked over to the guy's seat, something he rarely did. The guy was definitely gone though. Where were these people when he turned the tables, whenever things didn't go their way?

The bottom of the tenth turned out very quiet, in more ways than one. Besides the absence of noise coming from near the left field line, Terry entered the game and quickly retired the three Toronto batters, transforming the Oakland lead into a 6-4 victory.

"They're starting to call you *The Magician*," one of several reporters present told Rick Gonzalez.

"I'm no magician," Rick replied from the podium of the small interview room outside the visitors' clubhouse in Kansas City Stadium. "The guys have played hard and we've caught some breaks."

"Your team's nineteen and five since you became manager," another media person stated factually. "Eight and two on this road trip. Best one in ten years."

"Pitching's been good," was Rick's only comment.

But he did feel satisfied. Especially with the road trip, the final game of which had just ended, a 4-2 victory over Kansas City. He was looking forward to heading back to Oakland soon after this interview, to begin a ten game homestand following an off day tomorrow.

"Murdoch's been hitting," another journalist, this one bald, declared.

Rick nodded in agreement.

"That car incident," the bald man continued. "Hear anything more?"

"What's that got to do with anything?" Rick bristled.

"Sounds like the same old Murdoch...out late, and in trouble."

"Look," Rick answered angrily. "What I see is a guy doin' his job. Day in, day out. Healthy or injured. You guys realize he's played in more consecutive games than anyone in the league?"

"Maybe he's hitting," the bald man conjectured, clearly disregarding Rick's comments, "on account he wants to be traded to a contender."

"We're not far from being a contender ourselves," Rick replied, still angry.

He was correct. Today's win elevated Oakland to exactly .500, and into third place, only five games behind Texas, who led the division.

"Murdoch's your only big salary," the man persisted. "Any chance front office will get you another big salary or two before the trade deadline?"

"My business is what happens on the field," Rick declared. "Any other business I leave to front office."

Despite avoiding the question, Rick was quite sure he knew the answer. What you see is what you got. Management was interested in acquiring new players only if the result were lower salaries, not higher ones. And, as he'd theorized before about Murdoch, they wouldn't even keep *him* were not most of his contract being paid by Cleveland.

"I'm sure you wouldn't mind another player or two," the bald man countered.

"I like the guys I got," Rick stated. "Anyway, all this is purely speculation. Something I don't have time for right now because we have a plane to catch."

He had already started to leave the room before finishing the last remarks, unzipping his jersey top as he went.

CHAPTER TEN

The left hander, wearing a white uniform trimmed in blue, fired a fastball over the heart of the plate. The batter swung, but much too late. Strike three. Third out. The left hander trotted off the mound, toward the first base dugout.

Karen Riley, sitting in the grandstand, waved to him. So did little Tammy. Lauren Riley clapped her hands. Terry, seated next to her, on the other side from the two girls, could feel a wide grin cross his face. Billy Riley had just pitched his fifth scoreless inning. One more and he'd record a shutout.

"Told you he's got talent," Terry said to Lauren.

She smiled at him. He liked her smile, possibly because it conveyed a touch of shyness. He also liked sitting beside her, and had already caught himself glancing at her a couple of times during the afternoon, instead of at the game.

"He looks good in that uniform," he offered.

"He should," she chuckled. "He's had it a week and it's entirely replaced the rest of his wardrobe."

Terry grinned again. As he'd suggested to Billy, he had checked with several teammates about a good Little League. One of them knew a coach who lived near the Rileys. A couple of phone calls and Billy was on "The Dodgers," who played their games here at this park, close to the Rileys' house.

"I was sorry to hear about the children's father," Terry said carefully, once Billy returned to the mound for the final scheduled inning.

Lauren's only response was a solemn nod. Again, it wasn't the time or place to inquire further. He merely sat there silently, watching the game. Billy did give up two hits and a walk, loading the bases, but then managed to strike out the final two batters, securing his shutout.

53

"What happened?" Terry teased him as they all walked back to the house afterward. "Get tired out there that last inning?"

Billy, as usual, smiled shyly. Terry immediately recognized his mother's smile in his. Something he hadn't noticed before.

"Guess we'd better add a few wind sprints to our next workout," he winked.

This time, when they got to the white house, it was Karen who invited Terry inside, telling him that she and Lauren were baking a casserole for dinner.

"Sounds great," he said. "But I've got my own game to go to tonight."

"Mommy, can we go too?" Tammy bubbled.

"No sweetie. One game's enough for today."

Terry was feeling especially content as he left Oakland Stadium late at night, headed for Collie Quinn's car in the parking lot. Less than an hour ago he had struck out the final batter of the game with the tying run on third, notching his eleventh consecutive save as Oakland won 4-3. Every time Oakland had a tenuous lead in the ninth inning lately, a frequent occurrence in the last two or three weeks, Rick brought him in. No question he had solidified the closer role.

He spotted Collie's car ahead. Surprisingly, when he reached it, he found other players there. In fact, the entire Oakland infield was already seated in the car. Besides second baseman Collie behind the steering wheel, first baseman Phil Steiner, shortstop Felix Oates and third baseman Jack O'Rourke were in the back.

"Get in," Collie told Terry.

Terry did and Collie drove off, to the tune of a little laughter from the backseat. Why shouldn't there be, the way the team had been playing recently? Also, Terry knew that a beer or two in the locker room after a game was more rule than exception.

"Got us a little party to go to," O'Rourke informed Terry. "Hear the women flow even more than the wine."

"Groupies?" Terry asked a bit inanely.

"Plus some local talent," Steiner chipped in.

"Rather just go home," Terry requested, cognizant of being by far the oldest here, with the likelihood he'd get stuck with whomever the others didn't want.

"You're in the big leagues now, Rookie," was shortstop Oates's way of ending the discussion.

Collie seemed to emphasize that by driving nowhere near their neighborhood. In fact he started to ascend into hilly terrain. The roads became treacherous. Then they turned circular. For some reason, Terry flashed back to the old childhood game "ring around the rosy." He had no clue where they were as Collie stopped the car.

"Sorry, Rookie," O'Rourke announced. "Forgot to mention, you weren't invited to the party."

Terry suspected that he was being had; all four of the others getting out of the car provided further evidence. And when they opened his door and pulled him out, there was no doubt.

"Meant to bring you a road map, Rookie," Steiner said. "But we forgot it. Hope you got a good sense of direction."

Right after Steiner's comment, they *did* play ring around the rosy of sorts. They spun Terry in a circle three or four times. Then they laughed and got back into the car. Driving off, they shouted almost incoherently at him.

About the only words he could make out in their jumble were, "Have a good time, Gramps."

Rookies, according to long-standing unofficial big league protocol, didn't achieve any kind of recognized status with their respective teams until they had undergone some type of rite of passage. Terry knew that no matter how he performed on the field or what value he had for the team, he would sooner or later *get his*. Clearly, his teammates had taken advantage of his most obvious dependency on them, his constant need for transportation.

His earlier contentment when he left the stadium now changed to fear as he tried to figure out how to get home. He neither knew anyone in this hilly neighborhood, nor anything about the area. He assumed that his best option was to begin walking and hope he came upon something familiar.

But which way to start? He decided that whenever he had to choose a direction, he would pick the one leading downhill. They had driven a lot uphill, so his bungalow must be downhill. After beginning, he heard a dog barking in the distance, the way he was going. He considered that positive, since a dog would most likely be in a populated area, like his own neighborhood.

The night was getting cold and he zipped up the jacket he'd fortunately brought from the stadium. He passed a house with music and loud chatter coming from it and immediately thought of the party his teammates referred to. He had to laugh at himself for the thought, however. There was never a party; it was simply a ruse to dupe him. One that he'd fallen for, hook, line and sinker.

He continued downhill.   From the next block, or certainly nearby, he heard what sounded like a wolf. Or, maybe it was a coyote. Whichever, he walked very gingerly, as silently as he could.

Then finally, after stealthily negotiating another half mile or so, he came upon a vista situated above a deep canyon barely visible in the dark. He was able to see lights down below. There were plenty of houses in the distance and he spotted what was unmistakably an arterial.

Encouraged, he quickened his pace and actually started to jog.

Everything was becoming familiar to Terry. The shops and restaurants of downtown San Leandro. The outskirts of his own neighborhood. He even passed the exact place where he'd discovered Murdoch being attacked by the four thugs that night when the police became involved.

There had been no more news about Murdoch's car. Actually, he and Murdoch hadn't even spoken since the incident. Which made it all the more improbable—no, impossible—that Murdoch should drive by now, spot him walking and stop. Yet, that's exactly what happened.

"Get in," Murdoch instructed after opening his passenger door.

This was the second time that night that Terry had heard these words and he was much slower to react now. In fact, he glanced up and down the street, first looking for teammates and then for characters possibly following Murdoch. Seeing no one, he got into the front seat, and quickly noticed beside him a couple of items that looked like a fake beard and an orange hairpiece.

"So they found your car," he commented as Murdoch drove off.

"'Fraid so," Murdoch replied gruffly.

Terry was confused by Murdoch's response, since his car seemed both luxurious and in perfect condition.

"This is a rental," Murdoch addressed Terry's confusion. "Mine was completely stripped. Worthless."

"Oh...they get the guys?"

"Yep."

"Going to press charges?" Terry asked, a little anxiously.

"Nope."

"Why not?"

"Media'd crucify me."

Terry didn't reply.

"Anyway, those guys'd prob'ly press charges against me," Murdoch added. "Stealing their car."

"You didn't steal it. I did."

"Things have a way getting turned around. Next thing you know, I'm the one in court."

Murdoch had driven into the parking lot beneath the same apartment complex Rick lived in. Evidently Murdoch lived here too. Evidently, he didn't know Terry didn't. By then, because of his long walk and lateness of the hour, Terry was too tired to tell him.

Instead, he merely got out of the car, told Murdoch good night and managed the block or so back to his bungalow.

Before the homestand ended, Terry came to a decision. It was time he made arrangements for a car. Not a purchase, but a rental, as Murdoch had done. He went to an agency at the Oakland airport and selected a blue sedan. Though definitely nothing extravagant, much better than subways and buses.

His plan worked perfectly. He had use of the car for a couple of days (he took it to a museum and did some local sightseeing), then dropped it at the airport as the next road trip began, and made a reservation to pick it up again when the team returned to Oakland for the following homestand.

"Brass isn't happy," Rick Gonzalez told Terry, the two of them sitting in a little office outside the visitors' locker room at Tampa Bay Stadium.

"About what?" Terry asked, instantly defensive at Rick's tone.

"About some scrape you and Murdoch got in late one night."

Now alarmed, Terry didn't reply.

"They don't think there'll be any legal action," Rick said.

"Then what's the problem?"

"PR.... Something they don't take lightly."

Rick then asked him more about the incident, which apparently had come to the attention of management either via the police or the media. Providing as little detail as possible, Terry told him what happened. How he had discovered Murdoch being attacked. How he'd driven off in the assailants' car.

"Quick thinking," Rick commented.

"Felt more like reflex."

"It worked."

Terry simply shrugged.

"It's pretty common knowledge," Rick continued, "that Murdoch goes out late every night."

"No crime in that, is there?"

"Depends on what he's doing...any idea what he's doing?"

"None."

"Brass is very sensitive...they..."

But Rick was interrupted by a knock at the door. It was Clayton, Oakland's hitting coach, who stuck his head into the office to inform them the team was due on the field in five minutes for that night's pregame warm-ups. Then Clayton left.

"Heard Murdoch hits some pretty raunchy neighborhoods," Rick started up again. "Like he's in some kind of trouble. Or looking for some."

Terry didn't answer.

"Brass gave me a choice," Rick stated. "Either I get some answers or they will."

"You going to talk to him?"

"Murdoch doesn't talk to me."

"What then?"

"We tail him one night," Rick said softly, like he was a bit embarrassed.

"We?"

"I'll go to satisfy brass. You go 'cause you're at least a little involved."

"Might be dangerous," Terry replied, frowning.

Rick shrugged.

"Something else bothers me," Terry went on.

"What?"

"I've never known you to care what brass thinks."

"I don't," Rick answered quickly. "But I'm afraid if *we* don't do something, *they* will. And if he's in trouble, we might be able to help."

Terry nodded. There was another knock at the door. Clayton again. Time for pregame practice to begin. Terry and Rick got up and followed Clayton out of the room.

Oakland kept winning. Midway through the road trip they swept a doubleheader in Detroit, improving to five games above .500 and moving ahead of Seattle into second place in their division, only three and a half games behind Texas. Plus, in the wild card race (the second place team with the best record in each league qualified for the playoffs at the end of the season), they trailed only New York, by just two games.

Terry continued his fine pitching, recording his fourteenth straight save in the nightcap of the doubleheader. And Rick's magic with the young pitchers, especially Myong Lee Kwan, persisted. In fact, over the last thirty games, the pitching staff's combined earned run average was below 3.00, the best in the majors during that period.

But the big news was Murdoch's torrid hitting. It had become the talk of baseball. Since that first game in Seattle, he'd batted above .450, and his season's average climbed to .320. And near the end of the road trip, his consecutive game hitting streak reached thirty, the longest in the big leagues in more than three years.

Murdoch's name was now being mentioned in connection with Joe DiMaggio's long-standing record hitting streak of fifty-six games in a row.

CHAPTER ELEVEN

"I don't think he's after a hooker," Rick said while driving, he and Terry following Murdoch through a rundown Boston neighborhood. "Not when he could get practically any woman he wanted, without costing himself a penny."

"Maybe he doesn't want to risk any publicity," Terry replied.

"All some media guy'd have to do is spot him down here. He'd get plenty publicity."

"Maybe he doesn't care."

"But I care," Rick answered firmly. "Guy chasing DiMaggio's record... Chasing whatever he's chasing down here."

Terry merely shrugged, probably less at Rick's comment than at his own inane responses. Perhaps he could be excused though, because it was late, he was tired and didn't feel especially comfortable in this vicinity.

"Besides," Rick added. "He doesn't care if someone recognizes him, why the disguise?"

Terry couldn't disagree. Ten minutes ago they had come up behind Murdoch—like Rick, driving a rental car—and observed him wearing a brown pullover knit cap above a long dark wig. He looked much more like a strung-out poet or musician than the ballplayer who'd gotten a key ninth inning hit just an hour ago, in their 5-3 victory over Boston.

"He's not looking for drugs either," Rick said, sounding speculative.

"What makes you say that?"

"He'd have stopped and scored by now. Only profession outnumbering hookers around here is the drug dealers."

Terry had to agree. He'd seen them standing on practically every street corner. Police were also well represented. In a span of five minutes, he'd counted almost a dozen patrol cars.

"I'm sure you're the only manager in baseball that would be out here like this," Terry said.

Rick didn't answer right away. Terry noticed, even in the dark, a very serious expression cross his face. When Rick finally spoke, he sounded distant.

"This neighborhood's a little too familiar."

Unsure of his meaning, Terry didn't know how to react, so he remained silent. Besides, his attention was diverted by a large group of men in the middle of a block, huddled around a bonfire, obviously for warmth.

"When I was pitching," Rick continued, "arm troubles weren't my only problem."

"Drugs?" Terry guessed.

"Pain killers for my arm. Whatever I couldn't get from our team doctor."

"They sell pain killers down here?"

"They sell everything down here," Rick declared.

"Were they illegal?"

"No. Only thing illegal was I didn't have a prescription."

Terry shook his head, no doubt again more from his own ignorance than the information Rick had just imparted.

"I remember someone once bragging," Rick chuckled. "A famous movie actor or director, I think... That he could score whatever he needed in any U.S. city in forty-five minutes. I could do it in thirty."

Terry shook his head again.

"So," Rick went on, lowering his voice, "if Murdoch's got some problem, I'd like to help."

"Speaking of Murdoch," Terry said after a brief pause, "aren't you following him too close?"

Rick apparently hadn't noticed that he'd driven within a few yards of the back of Murdoch's car. He slowed down, letting another vehicle enter their lane, between their car and Murdoch's. Then he allowed Murdoch to gradually pull well ahead of them.

"Heard you're sponsoring a kid for Little League," Rick remarked a few minutes later.

"I helped get him on a team," Terry answered. "Saw him play the other day."

"Heard he's pretty good."

"Tossed a shutout."

"Bring him out to the stadium before one of our games," Rick suggested. "Like to see him pitch."

"You sure it's all right? Not against league rules?"

"I won't tell if you won't tell," Rick grinned. "Anyway...with brass so concerned about PR..."

They both laughed.

"Seriously," Rick continued. "Your involvement can make a big difference for a kid."

"Not just for the kid," Terry replied.

"Reminds me when I was young," Rick said a little sadly. "My dad used to play catch with me. When he came home every night, that's the first thing we did. I'd wait by the door..."

Terry didn't answer because he was thinking of his own father. And the impact his father had had on him.

"Forty years ago," Rick added, shaking his head, "and I still remember."

They were both silent several minutes while Murdoch continued leading them up and down streets of deteriorated Boston neighborhoods, with no apparent direction or destination. When again they came upon the same group of men surrounding the bonfire, it became evident he was even doubling back into areas he'd already covered. Eventually, he returned to their hotel parking lot.

"Better give him a few minutes," Terry suggested after Rick parked the car. "Before we go inside."

"Sure," Rick replied, removing the key from the ignition.

They waited ten minutes. As they walked from the parking lot to the hotel lobby, Terry couldn't avoid the irony of the last hour or so. They had set out to discover what Murdoch was doing late at night. The only discoveries Terry made, however, pertained to Rick.

"You guys out cruisin' tonight?" Murdoch asked Terry and Rick the instant they entered the lobby.

There was no one else present, except a lone desk clerk stationed on the other side of the huge room. Terry could see by his scowl that Murdoch, no longer wearing his disguise, wasn't happy. Neither he nor Rick replied to Murdoch's question. He hoped the expression on his own face didn't look as foolish as the one on Rick's.

"Or were you guys tailin' me?" Murdoch accused. "I doubled back on purpose...you were still there."

Again no reply, but Terry promptly remembered passing the bonfire twice.

"Can't claim you were there by accident. Neither you guys look the type to be chasin' what guys chase in that neighborhood..."

"Just seein' we could help," Rick mumbled, his foolish expression still present.

"Oh...I get it," Murdoch answered sarcastically. "Case I'm in some kind of trouble."

"Yeah," Rick muttered. "Case you're in some kind of trouble."

"Did it look like I was in trouble?"

"Just wanted to help," Terry managed, his meager contribution to the exchange no more convincing than Rick's.

"You *can* help," Murdoch declared. "By minding your own business."

Murdoch turned and, without glancing back at them, walked directly to a hotel elevator and stepped inside. As the door closed, Terry could see the scowl still on his face.

Terry was surprised when Rick called on the Oakland Stadium bullpen phone, asked that he warm up, and soon summoned him into the game. True, it was the ninth inning and the score was close—usual prerequisites to Terry entering a game. But tonight Oakland was behind, *not* ahead, trailing visitor Minnesota 2-1. Yes, the bases were loaded with none out, and obviously Rick wanted to avoid falling further behind. However, this wasn't a "save" situation. Terry was in a different role tonight.

When Terry got to the mound, Rick, catcher Bailey, and the entire infield were already there. Bailey left for home plate, to catch Terry's eight allotted warm-ups. Rick soon left for the dugout, though not before delivering a cogent message.

"Top of our order's up in the bottom half. Get 'em out and give us a chance."

All four infielders remained at the mound. As Terry tossed his first warm-up, he thought he heard a few snickers behind him. Clearly, they hadn't forgotten their little late-night escapade, with him as the target. Neither had he.

"You heard the skipper," first baseman Phil Steiner smirked. "Get 'em out and we'll win."

"Yeah," shortstop Felix Oates seconded. "I lead off, then Collie, and Murdoch, and Steiner, and O'Rourke. We'll scratch out coupla runs."

Terry couldn't help thinking, as Oates rattled off the names, that Oates had a future as a baseball broadcaster.

"We win," third baseman Jack O'Rourke contributed as Terry tossed his final warm-up, "got a party afterward. This time you're invited."

"No thanks," Terry muttered.

"Now, don't be a bad sport," Steiner mocked in a squeaky voice that sounded like a child's.

The four infielders laughed. Terry, of course, didn't. They returned to their positions. Bailey came out to the mound to quickly review signals, and then returned to behind the plate. The Minnesota batter, a righty who had already collected three hits, stepped into the box.

Terry fired his first pitch, a knuckler that dived low and outside for ball one. His next pitch, another knuckler, never reached the plate. Bailey blocked it with his chest protector. Ball two.

Terry took a deep breath and glanced at the runners leading off each base. He knew he had to come in or risk walking in a run. Bailey called for a fastball. Terry obliged. The batter was ready for it. He swung and smashed a low liner screaming toward left field. Oates took one step to his right at shortstop and dove headlong. The ball stuck in the webbing of his glove and didn't topple out when he hit the turf. One out.

The next batter, another righty, entered the box. Rick, in the dugout, signaled with his right arm for Terry to keep his wrist stiff. Terry concentrated on that for his first pitch, another knuckler. Except the prevailing wind in

Oakland Stadium wasn't blowing, and the "diver" didn't dive. The batter swung and blistered a grounder between short and third. This time it was O'Rourke who dove, headlong to his left.

His timing was perfect. He snagged the ball on its second hop. From his knees, he threw to Quinn at second base. The throw was in the dirt though, and Collie had to scoop it to record the force. As he pivoted to make the relay to first, the runner from first bore down on him. He slid into Collie, disrupting his throw. The ball hit the dirt about six feet in front of the stretching first baseman Steiner. He caught it in mid-hop while keeping his left foot on the bag. Double play, inning over, Minnesota hadn't scored. Rick led the dugout in offering high-fives to all the infielders.

Oates began the bottom of the ninth with a looping single to right center. Quinn sacrifice bunted him to second. Murdoch, who already had a single and double for the evening, was intentionally walked, even though it meant putting the potential winning run on base.

Steiner laced a single to right, the runners moving up a base. That left things up to O'Rourke, with the bases loaded, one out and Oakland still trailing by a run. For some reason he couldn't identify, Terry felt tenser than if he were pitching right now. He watched the Minnesota pitching coach go to the mound, and, following a brief exchange, return to his dugout without removing the pitcher.

O'Rourke took the first pitch, which was inside. He fouled the next pitch over the backstop behind home plate. He dribbled the ensuing pitch foul outside the third base line.

Finally, he got a pitch he could handle, a breaking ball that hung up in the zone. He drilled it, the ball kissing turf in left center. It rolled all the way to the wall. Oates and Murdoch easily scored the tying and winning runs, to cement a 3-2 Oakland victory.

Terry, elated, was the first to reach and hug O'Rourke, near second base. He didn't realize it at the time, but instead of a save, he'd just recorded his very first win as a major leaguer. What he did realize right then was how instrumental O'Rourke and his infield mates had been in the victory. Both defensively, in not allowing Minnesota to score off him, and offensively, with a slight assist from Murdoch, producing the winning rally.

"I'll go to the party," Terry had to shout to O'Rourke because by that time they were all surrounded by yelling, backslapping teammates.

Even with all the excitement, Terry was able to spot O'Rourke's wink in his direction.

CHAPTER TWELVE

"I think if you change your grip, Billy," Rick told the boy.

While standing next to him and Terry on the left field bullpen mound in Oakland Stadium, Rick demonstrated by taking the ball and gripping it across the seams. Then he placed Billy's hand the same way. Maple, the bullpen catcher Rick had recruited earlier, crouched and gave Billy a target with his glove. The youngster wound up and fired a fastball, hitting the target perfectly.

"Great, Billy," Rick praised.

The boy smiled his usual shy smile. Something he'd already done seemingly a dozen times since joining Terry and Rick on the field while Oakland players took batting practice. Clearly, Billy was thrilled to be there. Which in no way was diminished when Rick presented him with a new green and gold Oakland cap once they got to the bullpen.

It was well over an hour before the afternoon game with Anaheim was to begin, the second of a short homestand. Terry had wasted little time taking Rick up on his invitation to bring Billy out to the stadium. In fact, Terry had invited the entire Riley family, introducing them all to Rick prior to Billy going on the field. The workout had gone well, except for Billy experiencing brief periods of wildness, prompting Rick's suggesting the change in grip.

"Try one more, Billy," Rick said.

The boy fired and again hit Maple's target perfectly. Except this time the ball bounced off Maple's glove. Terry glanced at Rick, who winked back, indicating he recognized what Terry discovered during previous workouts with the boy—Billy's pitches had unusual movement.

Rick shook Billy's hand before Terry walked with the youngster to the gate leading to the grandstand, where Lauren, Karen and Tammy waited. Billy quickly showed them his new cap. Then, predictably, they were all bombarded by a horde of kids seeking autographs. Even Billy was asked to sign a few before the youngsters finally dispersed.

"I'm sure Billy didn't tell you," Lauren said to Terry once they were alone with only *her* children.

"What?"

"Today's his birthday."

"Really."

"We're having a little party later this afternoon. Just the kids and me at a pizza parlor near the house."

"Nice."

"Would you like to invite Terry?" she asked Billy.

The boy of course smiled, and then he nodded eagerly.

"Why don't you ask him?"

Billy kept smiling and nodding.

"Go ahead and ask him," Lauren said insistently.

"C...C...Come," the boy stammered.

"I'll be there," Terry answered enthusiastically, realizing this was the first time Billy had spoken in his presence.

"Mommy, can I have another piece of pizza?" Tammy enthused.

"Sure, honey, go ahead," Lauren replied.

"That's the last piece," Karen interjected. "It's for Mama."

"That's okay," Lauren said. "Let her eat it."

Five year old Tammy did, very quickly. Little girl, big appetite. Her brother, wearing his new cap, and sister had eaten plenty. Terry also. Only Lauren hadn't.

"Not very hungry?" Terry asked her.

"Pizza isn't my favorite dish."

"Let me get you something else."

"No thanks," she said. "They don't have much else here."

A nearby corner was devoted to video games, and their constant noise made hearing somewhat difficult. But of course, reminded patrons of their presence. Lauren took money from her purse and gave some to each of her children, who got up to go play.

"Great kids," Terry said to Lauren now that they were alone at their table.

"Thanks," she smiled.

The same shy smile he recalled from Billy's Little League game. He was also aware of her outfit—simple, yet attractive. Light-blue pants and blouse, with a matching sweater.

"You seem at home with children," he said.

"I should be...I'm always around them. My own kids and at work."

"Work?"

"I'm a social worker. In Texas I counseled teenagers. Mostly troubled kids from broken homes."

"Are you working here?"

"No," she answered after brief hesitation.

"Planning to?"

He wasn't sure of her reply. Partly because of the noise from the video games, partly because Tammy returned right then, interrupting them. No surprise, she had a stomach ache. Not that it kept her from ice cream after he suggested it, once Billy and Karen came back to the table.

A while later, sitting there with the Rileys, the children eating ice cream, Terry felt content—a sense of harmony and closeness, that he definitely belonged here—feelings he hadn't often experienced before. As the only child of much older parents, he'd spent a lot of time alone growing up. A circumstance that had persisted into adulthood.

It crossed his mind that he'd been lucky not to miss this little party. His game had run long, Oakland finally winning 6-5 in extra innings. If he'd had to depend on subways or buses, he'd have been too late. Fortunately, he'd followed through on his plan to rent a car after the road trip. And been able to easily locate the pizza parlor, from the directions Lauren had given him before she and the children left the stadium after Billy's workout.

"Billy checked out a library book," Karen told Terry once she finished her ice cream. "All about pitching."

"Oh?" Terry said.

"He wants you to come over our house and see it."

"Let Billy invite him himself," Lauren scolded her.

"Yeah, Billy," Karen retorted. "Invite him yourself."

The boy did nothing but smile.

"Go ahead, Billy," Karen urged.

"C...C...Come over," Billy mumbled, still smiling.

"Love to," Terry answered, aware Billy had just uttered twice as many words as earlier, at the stadium.

"I'm embarrassed," Terry admitted after Lauren sat down beside him on her living room couch and handed him a small green wrapped package.

"Why?" she asked.

"I can't accept a gift from you...when I didn't have time to get one for Billy."

"You gave him the new cap."

"That was from Rick. Not from me."

"I think you had something to do with it," she smiled. "You were the one who invited him to the stadium. *That* made his birthday special."

"But I didn't even know it was his birthday," he debated.

"Doesn't matter," she said. "What matters is what you did."

He shrugged. Then glanced around the room. The furniture was basic, even plain, yet seemed quite comfortable, chosen with care. If the little white house looked attractive externally, the inside certainly appeared very cozy.

They had arrived from the pizza parlor about dusk, more than two hours ago. Lauren had baked a cake for Billy, and she, Terry and the three children had eaten it in the kitchen, just as inviting. Then, before Lauren sent the children to their rooms to get ready for bed, Terry had sat down with Billy in the living room and looked through his book, a survey on baseball's greatest pitchers. Right after, requiring no less than equal time, Karen and Tammy insisted that Terry listen to some music tapes in their room.

"You're not going to make me open this now," he said, frowning, motioning toward the package, which he'd set down on the coffee table in front of him.

"No," she grinned. "You can wait till you get home."

He gazed at her during the brief ensuing silence. At her light-colored hair tied behind her with a turquoise ribbon. At her hazel eyes. At several freckles, which lent her face a youthful appearance.

Certainly he was aware professional baseball put extra strain on any relationship with a woman. All the travel, the moving, the uncertainty. Over the years, aside from the occasional groupie, he'd had two long-term relationships. The more recent, and more serious, with Connie three or four years ago, lasted through most of two seasons before she finally gave up. Maybe, if he'd made the majors then, instead of now?

"Billy likes it when you're around," Lauren spoke softly. "I think he gets tired being outnumbered by three females."

"That why he's so shy?" Terry inquired, finally taking the chance to introduce that topic. "Being outnumbered by the three of you."

"No, I don't think so. He's better with us. I think it has more to do with you."

"Me? Why?"

"You're a man."

Her reply startled him. What did gender have to do with it? Then, after reflecting a moment, he thought he understood. At least enough to hazard a guess.

"His father," he said, also trying to take advantage of what seemed a good opportunity to initiate that subject now too.

"Yes."

"They were close."

"Yes."

"His death..." he said carefully. "Was he sick?"

"No. Car accident. He was killed instantly."

He shook his head.

"And I'm afraid," she went on, "that Billy's afraid you'll disappear suddenly too."

"How long ago did it happen?"

"Two years. Billy was traumatized...and as you can see, to some extent, still is. All it takes is a connection to his father."

"And he connects me with his father?"

"Sure," she sounded definite. "You're male. About the same age...baseball..."

"Baseball?"

"The usual father-son stuff. Playing catch. Going to games. Watching on television. Listening over the radio. Discussing players and teams."

"What about the girls?" he asked. "Trauma too?"

"Not as bad for them. Tammy was very young. But they have their moments also."

"And for you...?" he asked carefully. "Must've been horrible..."

"I'm like Billy...I don't want to talk about it much either."

He could only shake his head again. He'd asked enough questions. And she'd answered them. Besides, he needed to let everything sink in. Plus, it was getting late; he'd had a long day and still faced the drive home.

And yet, sitting beside her, gazing at her again, he really didn't want to leave. Even in her sadness, she looked very pretty. He reached for her and pulled her gently toward him. Briefly, she nestled against his shoulder. Abruptly, she pulled away.

"Let's not," she said.

"I'm sorry."

"There are some more things you don't know."

"Oh," he said. "Want to tell me now?"

"No," she sighed. "Not now. I think we've had enough serious talk for one evening...don't you?"

He had to agree. He got up and she walked him to the door. Virtually at the same time, they both discovered that he'd left the green wrapped package on her coffee table. She went over, picked it up and gave it to him again.

He didn't wait until he got home to open it. In fact he hardly waited until he got to his car. Inside the green wrapping, he found a thick knitted woolen scarf, green and gold, of course Oakland team colors. In the dim street light, he was barely able to make out his name and baseball uniform Number 20 stitched into one corner.

Before driving off, he took one final glance at the little white house.

CHAPTER THIRTEEN

"You said you wanted to help," Murdoch declared.

Once Terry determined whose voice was coming through the phone in his hotel room, he was surprised. Not only because the hour was late, well past midnight, and he'd already gone to bed. No, after he and Rick were caught red handed by Murdoch a week and a half ago, he was sure Murdoch would never speak to him again. And, if he ever did, certainly not this soon.

Oakland was in Los Angeles for their initial interleague series. They'd played earlier that night, a 5-2 loss, their only runs coming on a pair of Murdoch homers. Extending his consecutive game hitting streak to forty-one.

"Well," Murdoch said, his tone clearly impatient. "You want to help? Or were you and Rick Gonzalez just blowin' smoke?"

"I'll help," Terry answered groggily. "What you want me to do?"

"Take a ride with me."

"Where to?"

"To Hollywood," Murdoch replied.

An hour later, riding through some much deteriorated territory, Terry had distinct feelings of déjà vu. Except this time Rick wasn't here. And he, Terry, wasn't tailing Murdoch; he was sitting beside him, as his passenger. Plus instead of Boston, they were in Los Angeles.

There was another difference. Though Murdoch was in disguise, it wasn't the same one. Tonight he was a chauffeur—at least from the waist up. He wore an elegant black sports coat, black tie, white embroidered dress shirt and black chauffeur's cap. Terry might have teased him about the outfit, except Murdoch looked so serious.

"Where we going?" he offered instead.

"Told you. To Hollywood. Where we are now."

"Why we here?"

"You'll see," Murdoch answered. "Maybe."

Since this line of questioning appeared futile, Terry tried a different approach.

"Hope you're not still mad at me."

"For what?" Murdoch responded, seemingly without interest.

"For that night in Boston. Rick and me following you."

"Was that Boston?"

Terry nodded.

"It wasn't your idea," Murdoch said.

"Not exactly."

"Then why should I be mad at you?"

"It wasn't exactly Rick's idea either."

"Whose was it then?"

Terry didn't answer.

"I know," Murdoch said. "Who else? Team brass…"

Terry remained silent. Not because of any sense of loyalty, but because of growing discomfort. Here he was in a desolate area, riding with a man he hardly knew. A man who definitely attracted trouble. A very large powerful man whom he suspected had a terrible temper.

"There," Murdoch suddenly said loudly.

Terry edged against the car door, trying to extend the space between them.

"There," Murdoch repeated, even louder, slowing the car.

"What?" Terry asked reflexively, barely aware that Murdoch had changed the subject.

"There. There she is…"

"Who?"

"Got a tip she was here," Murdoch said excitedly, disregarding Terry's question. "For once it's no wild goose."

Terry still had no idea what Murdoch was talking about. In the scant light, however, he did see a woman standing on the sidewalk, next to a tree, as Murdoch slowly drove past.

"This is where you come in," Murdoch stated as he pulled to a stop near the next intersection.

"Where?" Terry asked, still clueless.

"You go up to her," Murdoch explained, steering the car into a parking spot.

"Why me?"

"Cause if she recognizes me, she'll prob'ly just run. Raise a big commotion."

"What about your disguise?"

"Might not work."

Murdoch handed Terry the keys and instructed him to approach the woman and lead her back to the car. Meanwhile he, Murdoch, would walk up the street in the opposite direction. He would return once Terry had her inside the car. Then Terry would drive off.

"Isn't that kidnapping?" Terry asked nervously.

"I don't think anyone 'round here'll press charges, do you?" Murdoch replied, looking in his rearview mirror, apparently at the woman. "Now go ahead, before she goes away...and stop worrying."

But Terry wasn't at all reassured. Cast into this forsaken territory, he was about to participate in, even initiate, what was essentially a crime. For the *second* time in Murdoch's company. He glanced anxiously at Murdoch, who edged toward him, opened the passenger door and practically shoved him outside.

As he trudged away from the car, he looked back and saw Murdoch get out on the driver's side and begin walking the other way. Terry hoped the woman had gone by now. Then he could simply turn around, head back to the car, drive it to Murdoch and pick him up. All without doing anything illegal.

No such luck. The woman was still there, by the tree. As he drew closer, he saw she was tall, slim, black, casually dressed. And, a surprise, very young—perhaps only fifteen or sixteen.

"Hi," he greeted cautiously.

She looked at him, and then turned away.

"I know you don't know me," he continued.

"You alone?" she inquired curtly, turning back to him.

"Yes," he responded tensely, aware that his answer was less than truthful.

"You a cop?" she asked, again curtly.

"Hardly," he said, his voice cracking.

"Prove it."

"Come to the car and I will."

Evidently she believed him because she began walking with him. He knew he was at a crossroads. The only way he could excuse himself for allowing this situation to reach this stage was that Murdoch had awakened him from an intense sleep and he was still groggy. But now he was clearly leading this girl into a trap. A trap set by a potentially very dangerous man. Plus, they were apparently about to commit a crime, one that he was unmistakably participating in.

And yet, for some strange reason, he believed in Murdoch. That he wasn't about to harm this girl. That at some very deep level he could be trusted.

Nearing the car, he looked around for Murdoch. He didn't see him. Astonishingly, he found himself feeling warmly toward the girl beside him. Even in the minimal light, he could tell she was quite pretty, with smooth dark skin and pleasant eyes that seemed unusually bright.

From the passenger side, using the keys Murdoch had given him, he unlocked all four car doors and she got into the front. Walking around to the driver's side, he spotted Murdoch, still in disguise, coming toward them. As Terry entered the front, Murdoch slipped into the back.

"You said you were alone," the girl told Terry, accusingly.

Before he could reply, he noticed Murdoch take off his chauffeur's cap.

"Dad!" the girl exclaimed.

Before the following night's game in Los Angeles, Murdoch announced, through the team's Media Relations Director, that he would be declining the league's invitation to be Oakland's sole representative in this year's All Star Classic, less than two weeks away.

Media reaction was swift and intense. They claimed this was just one more example of Murdoch's arrogance and selfishness, his utter and complete disregard for the sport which supported him so handsomely. They pointed out that Murdoch hadn't missed a regular season game in over two years. For him to reject the All Star Classic could only be interpreted as a slap in the face to everyone involved in baseball, fans and players alike. Some even mentioned Murdoch's pursuit of Joe DiMaggio's record and how deleterious to the sport it would be if he broke it.

Murdoch, as he had done without exception in recent years, ignored all requests for interviews or a media conference.

"I think Murdoch found what he was looking for," Terry said to Rick.

"What?"

As the two of them sat off by themselves in the Los Angeles airport, waiting to board the team's flight back to Oakland, Terry told him about the events two nights ago. How he and Murdoch had driven to Hollywood. How they'd found Murdoch's daughter, Carly. How he'd then driven them to a different hotel than the team's. How he'd helped rent them a two bedroom suite there, for the duration of the series. How he'd gotten them reservations on a flight to Oakland, separate from the team's.

"That why he's not playing in the All Star Classic?" Rick inquired.

Terry looked at him questioningly.

"His daughter," Rick clarified.

"I don't know. He didn't say."

"Brass isn't happy about his declining the Classic."

Terry didn't reply.

"So," Rick went on, not looking too happy himself, "he finishes one big drama, then creates another."

CHAPTER FOURTEEN

"I don't need a babysitter," Carly told Murdoch as they sat on the couch in the living room of her new apartment, just down the hall from his.

"For sure," he responded.

"I won't be a prisoner, either."

"For sure," he repeated.

"You standing over me like I'm a little child."

"I'm not standing over you. Why you think I got you your own place?"

When she didn't answer right away, Murdoch glanced around the room. He was satisfied with the job management of the apartment complex had done. Furnishing it in soft pinks and yellows, rather than the dark colors dominating his place. They had even provided her a replica of the large yellowish-orange stuffed toy tiger that had been her constant companion when she was very young.

They'd accomplished this all on short notice. He had called them from Los Angeles yesterday morning and Carly moved in last night. All he had to do was sign the rental agreement and, of course, hand over his check, both of which he'd done earlier this evening.

"I think we need to face facts," she said sharply.

"What facts?"

"I got a little problem."

"What?"

"I think you know what."

"Drugs?"

Though she didn't reply, her expression confirmed his supposition. Not that he hadn't suspected while they were still in Los Angeles, because when he returned to their hotel suite after baseball, she'd either been asleep or acted very strange. Of course none of this made him happy. Nor did the way she looked—much thinner than when he last saw her before the other night, a little over a year ago. Plus, she had large dark circles under her eyes.

"No big surprise," he said. "Not with your mother's history."

"Don't think for a minute I'm going to detox," she responded, looking angry.

"No one's asking you to…. Unless you want to."

"I don't want to."

He didn't answer.

"I need my stuff," she declared.

"I don't want you on the streets, Carly."

"How you think it's going to get to me," she retorted, raising her voice. "Carrier pigeon?"

"You don't get what you need," he replied, raising his voice also, "you'll just run away again…right?"

"Right!"

"Then I don't have much choice," he said resignedly, in a lower tone. "I'll get it for you."

"You mean *you're* going to hit the streets!"

"No. I know some guys…they deliver. Anyway, the streets would be nothing new. Where you think I been all this time looking for you?"

She didn't answer right away. Her expression changed, becoming less severe. And when she did speak, her voice was much softer.

"Very expensive, Dad. All this."

He shrugged.

"New apartment. My shit…"

He shrugged again.

"I think you're asking for trouble," she said, her tone softer yet. "Having me around…"

"For me to decide," he answered firmly.

"You going to let Mama know?"

"Don't think so. Not right away."

This time it was Carly who shrugged.

"Unless you want me to," he added.

"I don't want you to…she'll just make more trouble for you."

"You haven't talked with her lately, have you…?"

"No," she said, practically whispering. "She has her own problems. Can't help me with mine."

80

"Where were you all this time?"

"Where you found me...the streets."

"Hollywood...? L.A...?"

"All over California, but mostly Texas."

"Texas?" he said grimacing. "What were you doing there?"

"Nothing you'd want to know," she replied, almost under her breath.

Heading down the hall to his own apartment later that night, Murdoch knew he'd done the right thing declining to play in the All Star Classic. With homestands coming up on both sides of the Classic, his next road trip wouldn't be for two weeks. Giving him time he needed right here.

During recent seasons, Murdoch received about a dozen letters a month, most of which could be categorized "hate mail." Many of these attacked his racial origin. Some accused him of abusing women, the specific evidence being—as reported by the media—his treatment of his ex-wife. Others, a very few now, came from Cleveland fans blaming him for their team's failure to achieve a World Series title.

The week before the All Star Classic, though, Murdoch's mail drastically increased, and not solely because of his refusal to play in the game. Or the perception that he was arrogant. Or overpaid. No, in the last game before the Classic, his ninth inning game-winning single raised his hitting streak to fifty, just six games short of DiMaggio's record.

Joe DiMaggio was an American hero, his death earlier that year getting front page headlines. Murdoch was his antithesis. If DiMaggio portrayed class, dignity, and pride, Murdoch was perceived as selfish, immature, and disrespectful.

The notion of Murdoch's name in the record books seemed universally distasteful. All the more if he replaced the great Joe DiMaggio.

"No way you guys stay in the pennant race."

This declaration, uttered by the elderly man sitting beside him on the airplane, caused Rick to laugh. He was in a good mood as they descended into San Diego. Taking advantage of the All Star break, he would be spending the next three days at the family home, visiting his two daughters who had time off themselves, from graduate school.

Like Rick, the elderly man possessed dark Hispanic features. Also like Rick, Rick later ascertained, the man had been involved with baseball many years—as a fan. Consequently, once he recognized Rick, as the Oakland manager, conversation was inevitable.

"You guys'll fade soon," the man continued.

"Thanks for the confidence." Rick grinned. "Maybe we should just cancel the rest of our season."

"Might as well, all the chance you got. Small market team..."

Rick didn't answer.

"Baseball's no longer a sport," the man went on. "It's a business. With only two sides, the *haves*, who can afford the best players, and the *have nots,* who can't."

Again, Rick didn't answer—though he did at least partly concur. Without doubt, economics were important. Teams with abundant finances could attract and keep player talent. And, no question, talented players were vital to success.

But the man's appraisal was far too simple. From Rick's perspective, it ignored a key ingredient. Possibility. Games were ultimately won or lost on the field. As long as that was true, nothing was predetermined. Possibility still existed.

Hadn't baseball always been a game of dreams? So much a part of the American psyche. Intertwined with the original American dream—with hard work, anything was possible. If possibility were removed, didn't the game lose much of its meaning?

"You've had a nice run," the man said, "for as long as it lasts."

At least Rick could agree on the first part of his statement—they had had a nice run. Murdoch's game-winning single yesterday lifted them to within two games of

Texas in the division race, and one and a half of New York for the wild card. The good pitching had continued, while Murdoch's hot bat sparked the offense.

"How long you followed baseball?" Rick asked, deliberately edging the conversation into slightly different terrain.

"All my life. Long before they ever dreamed bringing the big leagues out West."

"Guess you remember the old Coast League?"

"Sure...like it was yesterday," the man responded enthusiastically. "Those days, the game had heart and soul. Purity...magic...players played for love, not big money. And owners didn't rip off fans and cities."

"What about my team?" Rick asked, trying to establish something positive. "We've got heart and soul."

"Yeah," the man retorted, "but other than Murdoch, you got very little talent."

Rick didn't reply.

"Used to go to those Coast League games all the time," the man volunteered in a softer tone, perhaps aware of being a little harsh.

"Where?"

"Right here in San Diego," he answered, pointing toward the city, now in view from the airplane window.

"You don't recall the old ball park downtown? Near the bay?"

"Sure," the man said. "Went there all the time. You must've been a kid back then."

Indeed he was. Along with their nightly game of catch, Rick's father introduced him to professional baseball at the old ball park. In fact they attended doubleheaders there almost every Sunday the San Diego team was in town. And, like the man just did, his father often used words like "purity" and "magic" to describe the game.

"I'll be watching to see how you guys do," the man said as the plane was about to land.

"So we shouldn't just cancel the rest of our season?" Rick answered, managing a little chuckle.

"I think you got too much respect for the game to do that," the man stated.

Rick nodded. Finally, something on which they completely agreed.

CHAPTER FIFTEEN

"Did you go to school in Texas?" Terry asked Lauren, both of them sitting on her living room couch.

"College," she answered. "I went to the university. In Austin."

"I was wondering...why no accent?"

"You mean a gooood ole Ta-ax-is drawl," she mimicked, laughing, providing her own stellar rendition. "My family moved around a lot when I was young. Never long in one place."

"Are you close to your family?"

"Only to my brother. He lives here in San Francisco."

"Where does El Paso fit in?"

"I got my first job there. Right after college."

"In social work?"

She nodded.

"That where you met your husband?" he asked.

"Yes..."

But her voice tailed off. As if she didn't welcome this specific topic. He should have known. Especially recalling the sadness it caused her the last time, on Billy's birthday.

The situation now was pretty much the same as then. It was late evening and the children were in their rooms, although this time Lauren hadn't stipulated that they get ready for bed. All three were listening to radios—the girls to music and Billy to baseball, the All Star Classic. Terry had listened with him earlier, but with none of his teammates playing, his interest waned and he accepted Lauren's eventual invitation for coffee in the living room.

"Billy's talking to me more," he said, purposely changing the subject. "He actually spoke five or six sentences while we listened to the game."

"He's trusting you more," she answered.

"Trusting me?"

"That you're not going to suddenly disappear."

"But I haven't even seen him lately. Not since our last homestand."

"He *sees* you almost daily."

Terry, puzzled, didn't reply.

"On television...your games," she clarified. "If you're not playing, he even looks for you on the sideline."

He could only nod, not realizing he'd made such an impact on the boy.

"You're to be congratulated," she said after a brief pause.

"For what?" he asked, though certain she was about to compliment him on his ongoing pitching success. Or, the team's success.

"For taking us to do something not involving baseball. That helps him too. Helps him see there's more to you than just baseball. More to life."

He didn't reply. But, actually felt better than if she *had* complimented his pitching or the team. That afternoon, for the first time during any of his occasions with Lauren or the children, baseball hadn't been the central activity. In fact, in another first according to Lauren, Billy hadn't even worn his new Oakland baseball cap.

On the way home from his very first visit, Terry had noticed a small puppet theater near the subway station close to the Rileys. When he later called the theater, he was told matinees were offered every Tuesday during the summer. Today's performance had featured takeoffs on several current music stars, which of course appealed especially to Karen and Tammy.

"Let's check in on the kids," Lauren suggested, finishing her coffee. "I'll go see the girls...you, Billy."

"Sure."

When Terry entered Billy's room after knocking, the boy, now wearing his Oakland cap, was still listening to the game. He quickly smiled. But, Terry observed, not so shyly as in the past.

"Game almost over?" Terry asked.

Billy nodded.

"How we doing?"

"Losing," Billy answered, using careful pronunciation. "No Murdoch."

Terry grinned at Billy's explanation, and then went back to the living room couch. When Lauren returned, he noticed she looked tired. No doubt because they'd had a busy day—besides the puppet show, dinner at a nearby restaurant and a drive through some San Francisco hills offering scenic views of the city.

"Girls okay?" he inquired.

"Fine...Billy?"

"Good...except we're losing."

She smiled. Then she cocked her head and frowned. He could tell she was listening to something. Something from one of the kids' rooms, he assumed.

"That song," she said. "I used to sing it all the time."

They listened briefly. The music was obviously coming from Karen's and Tammy's room. He recognized the song as an old standard, "Fever."

"I used to sing it with a band," she explained.

"When?" he asked, a little surprised and confused. "I mean...when you weren't counseling?"

"Oh, no. Years ago. Back in college."

"Professionally?"

"I guess you could say that. But I wasn't good enough. I was a much better dancer."

"You danced professionally too?" he still sounded a little confused.

"No, no. Just for fun. We won a few contests...before Billy was born."

"What kind of dancing?"

"Oh...mostly swing."

"I'm impressed," he said, smiling.

"Thanks. But that was a long time ago."

She sighed. He could feel her sadness. Then, as if to erase the memory, she smiled. Wasn't this his chance to make another gesture toward intimacy? Maybe, like last time, put an arm around her and pull her close. Then see what happened...

"There are some more things you don't know."

Her words from their prior encounter came back to him. Clearly, she had something important to reveal. And yet, she'd introduced nothing he could point to, unless it was Billy's trusting him more or her talent as a singer and dancer. Which he seriously doubted. He sensed that if he made another attempt at intimacy right now, she'd simply rebuff him again, like last time.

Minutes later, at the door, after he'd said good bye to the children, she seemed disappointed he was leaving.

There were two outs and runners on first and second in the bottom of the eighth when Murdoch stepped into the batters' box. Oakland trailed Anaheim 4-3. Murdoch had gone hitless in three trips. With this plate appearance likely his last of the afternoon, the hitting streak, now at fifty-three, was in definite jeopardy.

Gazing out at Garth Williams, Anaheim's right handed set-up man, Murdoch was concerned. Not so much about the game. Or the streak. No, the homestand would end today, the team leaving for New York tomorrow, and it would be the first occasion since Carly reentered his life about two weeks ago that he'd be away from her for any length of time.

He'd actually considered not going to New York. Maybe request a few days personal leave from the team. Even retirement had entered his mind. But he knew by not going he'd only be attracting the media, who'd simply delve into every aspect of his life all over again—no doubt finding out about Carly and making her miserable too.

Besides, wasn't it time to let go a little? He couldn't always be so available to her. "Right down the hall," as he'd been lately. It just wasn't healthy for either of them not to have something of a life of their own.

Their two weeks together had been good, though. He had eaten with her at least once a day, either in his place or hers. Because neither of them welcomed being out in public any more than they had to, they avoided movies or concerts. Instead, Murdoch arranged for the delivery of film and music videos, through a distributor he knew. Also, there was always television and the new sound system in Carly's apartment, provided by management of the complex.

Murdoch, without question, had been concerned about her "little problem." About exactly what to do. Simply feeding her habit by procuring her "supply," as he'd promised, certainly wasn't his choice. But he sensed that, no matter how good their relationship, if he pressured her to stop or enter detox, she would merely rebel. Run away again, as she'd confirmed she'd do during their serious conversation about two weeks ago in her apartment. He therefore concluded that his best strategy was to go along with her for now, fulfill his promise, and see what happened.

Williams's first pitch was a slider, low and outside. Ball one. Murdoch knew he'd get nothing good to hit. Less because of the streak than the game being on the line. Why pitch to him in this spot—with an open base, trying to protect a one run lead?

Williams threw another slider, in precisely the same place, low and outside. Ball two. Murdoch couldn't help thinking this might be the best time for the streak to end. If he did manage to extend it, games fifty-five, fifty-six and fifty-seven would be in New York.

How ironic—a scenario of tying or breaking the record there, in DiMaggio's own home stadium. In front of tens of thousands of hostile New York fans. That part certainly appealed to him. But then there'd be the media. In the media capital of the world. They'd be swarming all over the place like flies. Making things unbearable for him, and for everyone else in Oakland uniform.

Williams fired another slider in exactly the same spot. Ball three. Evidently, the streak would end with a walk. Glaring at the big right hander, Murdoch wondered whether DiMaggio's last at bat in game fifty-seven had been a walk. Whether DiMaggio had gotten so much as a single good pitch to hit the entire day the great streak finally ended.

Many of the spectators began booing Williams. When he ambled behind the mound briefly, the noise level grew. Murdoch couldn't avoid smiling to himself. For one of the few times in his career, fans weren't booing him, but the opposition, on his behalf.

Williams didn't alter his tactics. One more slider, low and outside. Except this time Murdoch was ready. Stepping toward right field with his lead foot, the left, and reaching beyond home plate, he swung hard. Though the pitch was even farther outside and lower than the three previous, he did manage to make contact. But just barely. A weak fly, along the right field line. All the fielders, as usual, were swung around toward left, however, playing him to pull. The ball dropped fair by five feet. Both runners scored as Murdoch trotted into second with a double.

Once Terry retired the three Anaheim batters consecutively in the top of the ninth, Oakland had a 5-4 victory. And Murdoch's streak, now fifty-four, was still very much alive.

CHAPTER SIXTEEN

Even with all his years in baseball, Terry had never been to historic New York Stadium. Actually, he'd never been to New York. When he boarded the team bus for the stadium late in the afternoon, his teammates must have viewed him less as a ballplayer than an awestruck tourist. Neither the height of the buildings near their hotel nor the incredible noise volume of the city seemed possible.

Nor could he believe the stadium itself, once the bus arrived there. He found the outside magnificent, with its circular bluish-gray facade. However, the inside was even more remarkable. Like he had just discovered a wonderful oasis in the very heart of this gigantic metropolis. Walking across the field the first time, during pregame practice, he felt a delightful spring in his stride, as though the splendid green turf were really some form of rubber.

The game itself developed into a tight pitching duel, Terry watching from the bullpen beyond the left field wall. He became particularly focused whenever Murdoch came to bat, experiencing tension each time, as if he himself were hitting. Of course the capacity crowd strenuously booed each plate appearance, sounds Terry was certain carried for miles in the warm night air. But the boos quickly turned to cheers after Murdoch struck out, popped up and grounded out weakly in his first three tries.

New York led 3-2 when Murdoch came up in the top of the ninth. Once again, unless extra innings generated more plate appearances for him, his streak was on the line. Collie Quinn, the tying run, was at first with two outs. Terry expected New York to walk Murdoch. Or at the very least give him nothing good to hit. When Alfonso Carrasco, the right handed New York closer, poured the first pitch right down the middle, he was therefore surprised. Evidently, so was Murdoch, because he took it for a called strike.

The bullpen phone rang. It was Rick, instructing one of the bullpen catchers to tell him, Terry, to warm up, in case Oakland tied the game or went ahead, forcing a bottom of the ninth. Starting to throw, he didn't see the next pitch to Murdoch. He did hear the loud crack of the bat, though. And turned to see the New York left fielder heading his way, toward the wall. Then he heard another loud crack nearby, of the ball slamming against concrete.

The left fielder caught the carom after one brisk hop and hastily fired the ball to the shortstop, who quickly relayed it to the catcher. Quinn, dashing around the bases, attempting to tie the game on Murdoch's long hit, reached home plate simultaneously with the ball. A dusty cloud occurred, from Collie diving for the plate and the New York catcher diving for Quinn.

The umpire's right arm ascended. Quinn was out. The game was over and Oakland had lost. But Murdoch's streak was now fifty-five.

Just one more hit tomorrow and he'd equal the great DiMaggio.

Murdoch was awakened by a loud knock at his hotel room door. Without turning on a light, he glanced at the clock near the bed. It was almost 2:00 a.m. Who could be knocking now? He'd left his usual instructions with the hotel desk—no phone calls (except from Carly), no visitors.

There was another loud knock. And shuffling of feet from the corridor outside his door. Then a voice.

"Murdoch. I'm sorry. You there?"

"Who is it?" Murdoch asked angrily.

"Rick...Rick Gonzalez. We got a problem."

Murdoch turned the night table lamp on, got out of bed, located a bathrobe and put it on over his naked body. As he made his way to the door, there was another knock.

"Yeah...what's the problem?" he uttered.

"Police captain's with me," Rick answered. "Can we come in?"

Murdoch opened the door only as far as allowed by the chain lock he had attached earlier. After confirming it was Rick, he unhooked the chain, opened the door wider and stepped aside. Rick entered the room along with another man—early fifties, heavy, wearing sports coat and tie, flashing a police badge. Murdoch nodded toward two chairs in a corner of the room and the two men sat down while he remained standing near the door.

"Strader...New York Police Department," the man said, New York accent evident. "Can I get right to the point?"

"Yeah," Murdoch responded. "Wish you would."

"Since you got here, we received six death threats."

"On me?" Murdoch asked.

"On you."

Murdoch didn't reply.

"Some of them are obvious hoaxes," the police captain continued. "But we're taking two very serious."

Again Murdoch didn't reply.

"One of them mentioned your daughter."

"My daughter!" Murdoch exclaimed. "How they know about my daughter?"

"Sometimes some of them know a lot. Those are the ones we take serious."

Once more Murdoch didn't answer.

"I'll get to the point again..." Strader said. "We don't think you should play tomorrow or the next day."

"Don't play..." Murdoch said, practically under his breath.

"Right. You make an easy target out there in left field."

"You think someone's gonna shoot me..."

"There'll be fifty thousand people, and you know New York. Some of them'll be crazies."

Almost as if for effect, a door slammed loudly down the hall, causing all three men to glance in that direction. A brief silence followed, like they expected something else to happen. When nothing did, it was Rick who resumed the conversation.

"Hate to see you out of the lineup...but I think it's best."

"Haven't missed a regular game...more than two years," Murdoch muttered. "And what about the streak?"

"Break it in our park in a couple days," Rick said. "Brass'll love you. All the extra tickets they'll sell."

"Our fans aren't exactly hospitable either," Murdoch stated.

"Maybe," Strader interjected. "But nothing like New York."

Murdoch thought. No, this wasn't his way. Letting himself be bullied. Cowering from some random threats. He was a ballplayer. That was his job. In good weather or bad, healthy or not, he played...

"No," he said.

"No, what?" Strader responded.

"I'm not sitting out."

"At least let me DH you," Rick offered. "Keep you from being an easy target out there all night long."

"No," Murdoch declared. "I'm the left fielder."

Once Rick and the police captain left, Murdoch went straight to the phone in his room and dialed Carly's number. 2:00 a.m. in New York was 11:00 p.m. in California. She might not have gone to bed yet. He had called earlier, right after getting back to the hotel from the stadium, but she hadn't answered. Following several rings now, he became concerned. Where was she? And then she finally picked up.

"Where were you earlier?" he asked once they'd exchanged greetings, hers sounding sleepy.

"I went out for a walk after your game on TV. Got a little air."

"Oh."

"Dad, you worry too much."

"That guy delivering your stuff?"

"Perfect," she answered cheerily. "Like clockwork."

"Told you I'd take care of it."

"Thanks, Dad."

She *should* thank him, considering the sum he was paying. He'd been aware delivery costs were high, but this was outrageous. Probably taking advantage because it was him. Good thing he was making the money he was making. Anyway, what was the alternative? Other than picking up her supply himself.

"You staying in the rest of the night?" he asked.

"You worry too much, Dad."

"Carly...stay in the rest of the night. Don't go anywhere."

94

"Okay, okay."
"See you in a couple days, honey."
"Couple days." she said before hanging up.

CHAPTER SEVENTEEN

Rick was having a terrible game. Not because Oakland was losing—they weren't. Or that Myong Lee Kwan, the starter, had pitched badly—he hadn't. Or that they were playing poorly—actually this might have been their best defensive performance of the season, featuring an assortment of great plays, at almost every position. In fact, artistically, it had been a terrific game, now tied 2-2 entering the ninth.

Simply put, Rick's problem was Murdoch. Every time Rick heard an unusually loud noise, he immediately looked toward left field. Was Murdoch okay? Or had some New York crazy done something crazy? In the second inning he heard a loud cracking sound, like a gunshot. He was sure he had seen Murdoch flinch, like he'd been struck, but it turned out to be nothing more than his own imagination.

If Rick agonized over Murdoch's safety all evening, he certainly found no solace in New York's strategy toward him, Murdoch. To prevent his tying DiMaggio's record. They had thrown him sixteen consecutive pitches nowhere near the strike zone. His only contact came when he swung at a 3-0 slider in the dirt and grounded out sharply to the third baseman. Scheduled to bat fourth in the top of the ninth, he might not get another opportunity. Unless of course Oakland mounted some type of threat, or the game went extra innings.

The first batter, catcher Bailey, lined a single to center. Oates, the shortstop, after fouling off two bunt attempts, hit a double play grounder to the New York second baseman. He bobbled it, though, and both runners were safe.

After New York brought in their closer, Carrasco, Rick considered instructing the next batter, Collie Quinn, to bunt. If Quinn sacrificed successfully, however, advancing the runners to second and third with one out, New York would no doubt once more deliberately walk Murdoch, the following hitter. Rick did flash a series of signs to Clayton, coaching at third, but none of them meant anything, meaning Collie was to swing away. When Carrasco's very first pitch grazed Quinn's jersey, entitling him to first base, Rick couldn't believe their good fortune. Bases loaded, none out, game tied, Murdoch coming to the plate. They'd have to pitch to him now, wouldn't they?

Stepping into the batters' box, Murdoch couldn't believe the good fortune either. In this situation, Carrasco would have to give him something to hit. Something he could drive, enabling him to keep the streak alive, and break the 2-2 tie.

Murdoch looked out at Carrasco on the pitching surface and noticed he appeared confused. In fact Carrasco glanced repeatedly into the New York dugout, as if seeking instruction. Or wanting someone to come to the mound and offer clarification. But no one came.

He fired his first pitch, a big overhand curve, very low and outside. Ball one. Seventeen consecutive pitches nowhere near the strike zone. Murdoch shook his head. New York, an organization with so much history and tradition, taking this cowardly approach to protect the record of one of its former stars.

Last night, after Rick and the police captain left, Murdoch had trouble falling back asleep—not because of the streak or any fear the death threats aroused about his own safety. No, he was worried about Carly. The fact Strader had implied she was in jeopardy. And he, Murdoch, was three thousand miles away, powerless should anything happen.

He had phoned her twice more this morning. Waking her both times. But she'd been fine, in good spirits, even chiding him again for being overprotective.

To counteract his insomnia, he'd tried some late-night television, hoping it would make him drowsy. A futile attempt. He could find nothing of interest except sports. And seemingly, every time he switched channels, someone brought up the streak.

One commentator labeled DiMaggio's achievement the last great baseball record. He pointed out that in recent years Mark McGwire had shattered Roger Maris's home run standard, and Cal Ripken Jr. snapped Lou Gehrig's consecutive games played streak. Now DiMaggio's was the only venerable record that remained. Enduring more than half a century.

The commentator also managed to work Babe Ruth into his essay. And the fact that Ruth, Maris, Gehrig and of course DiMaggio all played for New York. Standing there at home plate, Murdoch couldn't fathom a team with such rich tradition doing what they now were doing.

Carrasco's next pitch, another curve, was even lower and farther outside. Ball two. Murdoch could only shake his head again. A deliberate walk with the bases loaded in a tie game?

What would the media say about this? Would they attack the New York team for its utter lack of integrity? Or applaud them for preventing someone like him from tying the record?

Murdoch had been right about the media swarm here in New York. Making everyone's life miserable. And he knew it would only get worse tomorrow, if he somehow managed a hit today.

Carrasco glanced at the New York dugout again. Then he fired. Another curve. Farther from the strike zone than the previous two. Ball three.

As Carrasco looked at the New York dugout once more, Murdoch, out of habit, glanced at third base coach Clayton. No way would Clayton give him the "take" sign. Not in this spot, with so much at stake. Clayton grabbed his belt with his right hand—the "hit" sign.

Murdoch had an idea. Anticipating another pitch low and outside, he would step toward right field and reach beyond the plate, as he'd done against Anaheim in the final game of the homestand to keep the streak alive. Carrasco fired again. A fastball, high and inside, directly at Murdoch's head. There was no way he could hit it.

In fact, it would have hit *him* had he not dropped quickly to the ground.

*****

98

On the flight back to Oakland late the next night, Rick sat near the rear, alone. Not that he would have minded some company. But the entire New York series had been so draining that he, like seemingly everyone else on the team, preferred to catch up on sleep.

Eyes closed, he wondered if he felt worse about Murdoch not equaling the record, or that they had lost two out of three. No question, Murdoch. Actually he felt pretty good about the team. Without doubt, they had accounted themselves well. Challenging New York throughout. All three games decided by one run. And the two they lost—when Collie Quinn got thrown out at the plate in the first game, and earlier tonight—they could have won.

Tonight's game probably shouldn't have been played. And probably wouldn't were it not their final scheduled appearance in New York for the year. A heavy downpour delayed the start more than an hour. And a steady drizzle fell during the rest of the evening.

Ironically, the night after his streak ended, Murdoch drove in all five Oakland runs with five consecutive hits. But, he also contributed significantly to the loss, losing a fly ball in the lights with the bases loaded in the eighth inning. The three baserunners scored, turning a 5-3 Oakland lead into a 6-5 deficit they couldn't overcome.

Besides feeling pretty good about his team, Rick felt very relieved they were leaving New York without Murdoch being harmed. Rick had checked with Police Captain Strader about four o'clock and learned there were no more death threats. The two Strader took seriously both mentioned the hitting streak. And now that it had ended and they were returning to California, Strader speculated that the danger had diminished.

Sitting there in the airplane, Rick suddenly found himself shaking his head, still unable to reconcile New York's methods in aborting Murdoch's streak the previous night. Save DiMaggio's record, even if it cost them the game. And it had, the deliberate walk with the bases loaded forcing in what ultimately became the winning run.

What had baseball come to? Where was the integrity? In a game with potential wild card implications, one team had, in essence, let the other team win. Did New York take them that lightly? That they could afford to give them a game and not have it matter in the final standings.

The standings—that's where his thoughts turned next. Oakland had fallen to three and a half behind Texas in the division and three behind New York for the wild card. Maybe the elderly man he had encountered on the flight to San Diego was right. That they soon would drop out of contention. That a small market team really couldn't compete.

But Rick liked his team. The solid pitching, good defense...and Murdoch. Of course it would be nice to add a player or two, especially a power hitter who could follow Murdoch in the lineup. Someone who might protect him a little, keep opponents from simply pitching around him so often. With the July 31 trade deadline only about a week away, Rick made a mental note to discuss some possibilities with front office.

This was often the time when teams in the pennant race offered future prospects to teams no longer in contention, in exchange for established players, thereby strengthening themselves for the final two months of the season. Non-contenders benefited by cutting current payroll, while hopefully enhancing their future.

Unfortunately, Rick sensed what front office's reaction would be. The budget. Make do with the players they had. Unless he wanted to acquire more prospects for an established player. Murdoch, to be specific. Which, of course, he didn't.

He could debate that their main competition would improve themselves—Texas, for example, its pitching; New York, infield and bench. But his argument probably would have no impact. Not if it increased costs.

He must have fallen asleep, because his next conscious awareness was of the plane taxiing toward the arrival gate. Perhaps expressing relief that New York was no more than a distant memory, he took a deep breath. Then he glanced at his watch. 5:00 a.m. Really 2:00 a.m. Oakland time.

The team had an off day tomorrow. Actually today. Good thing...he could use one.

CHAPTER EIGHTEEN

"No one else I can call."

This time Terry was quickly able to identify the voice coming through the telephone in his bungalow. Who except Murdoch had called very late at night recently? This time, unlike the prior, when Murdoch summoned his help in Los Angeles to locate his daughter, Terry wasn't asleep. In fact, he wasn't even in bed, since he'd just arrived from the airport, where it had taken longer than usual to rent a car.

"What's the matter?" he asked.

"Carly..." Murdoch replied, his voice sounding strange. "Meet me...hospital."

"Which hospital?" Terry inquired, now alarmed.

"Near..."

Terry assumed he meant the one less than a mile away, which he remembered from one of his walks.

"I'll be there in five minutes," he said. "Where do we meet?"

"'Mergency room," Murdoch mumbled, and then hung up.

Approaching Murdoch, who was standing in a corner of the emergency room, Terry saw he wasn't wearing one of his disguises. Though it almost seemed as if he was. Clothes mussed, badly needing a shave, face dirty, hair unkempt. Looking very much like Terry felt, this late at night.

"Where is she?" Terry asked.

"Already...took her," Murdoch muttered.

"What is it?"

"Expectin' somethin'. Not this."

"What is it?" Terry repeated, more emphatically.

Murdoch, appearing practically in shock, didn't answer.

"What's wrong with her?" Terry said, now very alarmed.

Again Murdoch didn't answer, this time merely shrugging. Terry noticed his upper lip begin to quiver. And his left hand shaking. In fact, he seemed far more nervous, even out of control, than at any time during the long streak.

"O.D.?" Terry guessed.

Murdoch nodded, almost imperceptibly.

"Can we see her?"

"They want us...register her," Murdoch said, barely above a whisper. "Told them...wait for you."

Terry didn't answer.

"Media find out...she my daughter..." Murdoch continued, rambling almost incoherently. "Crucify me. Her too. Swarm 'round here...like flies"

"I'll register her," Terry said, surprised at his own words.

"Don't think they let you..."

"Let me try," Terry replied, beginning to edge toward what he assumed was the admissions office.

"How is she?" Terry, still alarmed, asked the doctor, a thin man in his mid forties, who had just entered Carly's hospital room and was now taking her pulse.

"Seen worse."

Standing near Murdoch, beside Carly's bed, Terry didn't know how the doctor could say that. Not unless he was comparing her to patients already deceased. Which, when first coming into the room, Terry had feared was precisely her status. Then he'd observed the barely perceptible movement of her upper body as she breathed. She looked terribly pale, gaunt. As if, rather than an ordinary hospital room, she belonged in the intensive care unit. Where, he later learned, she'd been initially taken.

"She be okay?" Murdoch tensely asked the doctor.

"She's not out of the woods yet."

"Anything we can do?" Terry inquired.

"Yeah, keep her away from that stuff. Next time she might not make it this far."

After writing some notations on a clipboard he was holding, the doctor departed, leaving Terry and Murdoch by themselves to stand vigil. Apparently, Murdoch had visited a restroom, because he looked much better than earlier. While he still needed a shave, his face was clean and his clothing straighter.

"That damn streak..." he said solemnly. "Glad it's over. Don't think she could handle it...all that publicity."

Terry nodded. But his thoughts were elsewhere. Back to the admissions office, where less than an hour ago he'd managed to get Carly officially admitted without implicating Murdoch—by telling several lies. Her last name became his, Landers. Her address was his bungalow. Due to the recent marriage between her father and his step sister, he'd just become her uncle. No, he knew nothing of any drug use. He'd discovered her comatose after returning from a business trip (he didn't even want to acknowledge being a ballplayer, because of the possible connection with Murdoch).

He nearly smiled now at his own creativity. If admissions personnel believed any of what he'd said, he had no idea why. Unless, of course, at that time of night, no one really cared. Or the graveyard shift didn't attract the most competent people.

"I ever need a witness to vouch for me," Murdoch remarked much later, after he'd had a chance to regain his composure and Terry told him some of his story, "you get the nod."

Terry grinned at Murdoch's comment. Then he noticed the initial light of dawn filtering into the room. Fortunately, their next game wasn't until tomorrow night.

"What's the name of that old movie?" Terry asked Lauren as they sat in their regular place, on her living room couch. "Around the World in Eighty Days?"

"I think so," she answered.

"Feels like I've been around it twice in the last four days."

"New York can do that to you," she smiled.

"So can spending half the night in a hospital."

No doubt he'd used the film analogy because a movie had been the evening's principal activity. An animated movie based on a Greek myth, thoroughly enjoyed by the children. They'd all had dinner in a Chinese restaurant before, and after, tackled a picture puzzle of several famous women that Lauren had bought for the girls. By the time they finished, it was nearly eleven and she sent the children to bed.

No question he'd just mentioned the hospital because it was very much on his mind. He then told her about the drug overdose. How Murdoch had summoned his help. How he'd tried to nap several times today, without much success, before this evening's activities.

"Sounds like some of my nights in Texas," she said. "I worked with a lot of runaways there...never knew what they were going to do."

"Murdoch's daughter was a runaway."

"Oh?" she replied, looking surprised.

"We found her on the streets of Hollywood."

"Oh?" she repeated, still looking surprised. "What's her name?"

"Carly."

"Carly Murdoch?" she asked, raising her eyelids, as though possibly recognizing the name.

"Yes," he answered after pausing briefly, recalling he'd renamed her Landers late last night.

"Describe her."

"Tall. Slim. Maybe fifteen or sixteen."

"Pretty?"

"Very."

"This may sound strange," she said. "But I worked with a Carly in Texas. She used a different last name. Said her father was a famous ballplayer. I'm not sure I believed her —these kids say anything. Called him Mr. Ten Million."

"Murdoch's salary..."

"This girl was pregnant..."

"I wouldn't know about that," he replied.

"Of course not.... But it sure sounds like it could be her."

"Wouldn't be hard to find out," he said. "I told Murdoch I'd meet him at the hospital tomorrow. You could come too."

She frowned. As if he'd said something objectionable.

"What time?" she asked.

"About one."

"Okay," she said softly. "I'll meet you there."

He gave her directions to the hospital, which she wrote into a little tan notebook. When she stopped writing, he tried to stifle a yawn.

"Guess I'd better be going," he said. "Unless your couch is available for the night."

"No," she quickly countered. "The kids might not know what to think...in the morning."

"That the only reason?"

"No," she answered, not as quickly.

"Want to talk about it now?"

"No, not now. Soon."

"Promise?"

"I promise," she said, getting up to walk him to the door after he tried to stifle another yawn.

Consistent with the theme of the last few days, Terry was having an active morning. Besides running a couple of errands and calling Murdoch to get an update on Carly (no change) and to make sure it was okay for him, Terry, to bring Lauren to the hospital that afternoon (some resistance, but ultimately relenting), he was now signing autographs at an indoor shopping mall a few miles south of Oakland. It was a charity event, whereby the mall association donated ten dollars per autograph to a cluster of local charities.

Despite the impingement on his time, Terry was quite thrilled to be there. Especially when many of the mall patrons addressed him as Mr. Closer, or a similar epithet. The occasion reminded him of the times he'd played mall Santa Claus at Christmas-time during his minor league days (even though he was far from being portly).

He was also thrilled by the amount of fan mail he'd received lately via the Oakland team public relations department. True, it was time-consuming, but he tried to answer each letter personally. And was further delighted when some of the correspondents answered his letter with another of their own.

By far the highlight of the morning was the arrival of a busload of students from a nearby school for handicapped children. Terry took extra time with them, carefully spelling out their first and last names as a salutation for his autograph.

Entering Carly's hospital room with Lauren, Terry was puzzled that Murdoch, there already, was again in disguise. He was wearing the same one he wore that night in Boston when Terry and Rick tailed him. Brown pullover knit cap above a long dark wig, making him look more like a strung-out musician than an apprehensive father visiting his daughter.

"How is she?" Terry asked him after introducing Lauren.

"Same," he said despondently.

Terry nodded. She certainly looked the same as early yesterday, after he'd completed the admission process. Pale, gaunt, lifeless. He glanced at Lauren. Her expression conveyed concern. It also inferred, from the look in her eyes, that she knew her.

They stood there a few minutes before Murdoch, seeming far more focused than early yesterday, motioned them outside the room, into the corridor. Once there, Terry briefly explained to Lauren Murdoch's purpose for disguise.

"Who are you?" Terry then asked him a little awkwardly.

"Starving artist," Murdoch muttered, looking a little sheepish.

"No... I mean... I hope you didn't tell anyone around here you're her father."

"No. Her uncle."

"But I'm her uncle," Terry disputed.

"Nothing for the two of you to quarrel over," Lauren interjected.

Terry and Murdoch looked at her questioningly.

"You can both be her uncle," she said, beginning to grin. "A person can have more than one."

Despite Carly's circumstances, Terry and Murdoch each laughed. No doubt primarily because they were embarrassed by their own ignorance. Lauren laughed too. Then she mentioned her children, whom she'd left in the hospital lobby, where she and Terry had met twenty minutes ago. After saying good bye to Murdoch, they began walking back there.

"You know her," Terry said.

"Yes. She's the girl we spoke of."

"Will she recover?"

"Yes, I think so.... The first several hours are always the most crucial."

"You know a lot about this stuff."

"I'm afraid so," she said. "Most of the kids I worked with were on drugs. Especially the runaways."

"You said she was pregnant."

"She was."

"What happened?"

"She had the baby. Gave it up for adoption. Then, ran away again, pretty much according to pattern."

"I guess that's where Murdoch and I came in," he remarked. "When we found her in Hollywood."

She didn't answer, undoubtedly because they had reached the lobby. The three children spotted them and headed their way. Little Tammy immediately wanted to know if they could all go to a puppet show or a movie or a restaurant. Lauren told her she was sure Terry had a game later, and couldn't.

"Mommy," Tammy said eagerly. "Can we go see Terry's game later?"

"No, sweetie. Let's save it for another day. We've got a long drive ahead."

"Thanks for coming," Terry told Lauren.

"I'll stay in touch with the hospital."

He nodded. Then he walked with them to their car and watched them drive off.

CHAPTER NINETEEN

Terry was startled when the bullpen phone rang. Myong Lee Kwan, who'd accompanied him in the trade more than two months ago, had pitched masterfully all afternoon, surrendering just two hits. Oakland was batting in the bottom of the eighth, leading San Francisco 1-0 in an interleague game.

"Get warm," one of the bullpen catchers instructed Terry after hanging up the phone.

"You sure?"

"What the man said," the catcher replied, obviously referring to Rick in the dugout.

Terry shrugged, then got up and began throwing. It made no sense. Kwan's pitch count was low, under a hundred. And the young right hander—whom Terry recently learned was a U.S. citizen by birth, his father coming to this country from Taiwan, his mother from Mainland China—had a shutout, something Rick liked giving his starters every opportunity to complete. Consequently, when minutes later Kwan returned to the mound to begin the ninth, it was only logical. Terry sat down, still wondering why he'd been asked to get up in the first place. But then, after Kwan tossed a couple of warm-ups, Rick emerged from the dugout and motioned to Terry.

"Changed my mind," Rick said once Terry trotted to the mound and Kwan left for the dugout.

"Didn't expect this," Terry replied, rubbing up the baseball Rick had just handed him.

"Why? You're the closer."

"He had a shutout."

"You're the closer," Rick repeated before leaving for the dugout.

Terry started his warm-ups. He was seeking his twentieth consecutive save. One of his teammates, probably Collie Quinn, had mentioned he thought he read where twenty-five was a record for a rookie at the outset of his career in the majors. But Terry had paid little attention, likely because of having difficulty reconciling the term "rookie" with age thirty-three.

The San Francisco leadoff hitter, a lefty, drilled Terry's first pitch up the alley in right center, for a double. The next batter sacrifice bunted back to Terry, who tossed to second baseman Quinn, covering first. One out, tying run advancing to third.

The number three man in the San Francisco lineup, the dangerous Lathan, strode toward the right hand batters' box. Terry could feel himself perspiring. The afternoon was perhaps the warmest he'd encountered here so far. Of course reminding him of Texas. And of course how terribly he'd performed there, before Rick straightened him out.

The infielders edged in, hoping to prevent the runner scoring on a grounder. With two bases open, Terry knew the strategy was to pitch very carefully to Lathan. He tried to throw "the diver" low and away. It caught too much of the plate, however. Lathan swung, ripping a liner over shortstop Oates's head. Terry slumped almost to his knees, sure he'd given up the tying run, ruined Kwan's shutout and blown the save.

Evidently, Murdoch wasn't so sure. He rushed in from left field as the ball carried toward him in the warm air. Diving headlong, left arm and glove fully extended in front of his big body, he caught the ball a split second before both he and it fell to the green turf.

The runner at third committed a major blunder. Apparently certain the ball would land in front of Murdoch, he ran toward home plate instead of immediately tagging up. By the time the runner recognized his mistake, Murdoch scrambled to his feet. He fired a perfect strike to third baseman O'Rourke, who stepped on the bag well before the runner.

It was a double play, the game was over, Oakland had won, the shutout was preserved and Terry had his twentieth straight save. But just barely—on all five counts.

"Never thanked you," Murdoch greeted Terry in the corridor outside Carly's hospital room the next afternoon.

"For what?"

"For saving my ass again...getting Carly admitted without implicating me."

"And I never thanked you," Terry retorted. "For saving my ass again...with that great catch."

"How 'bout the throw?" Murdoch grinned.

"The throw too..."

Murdoch laughed. The truth was Terry couldn't ever recall him looking this happy. Then he realized something else. This was one of the few times he could remember seeing Murdoch dressed nicely in public, wearing normal street clothes, with no disguise.

"Don't care if they recognize you..." Terry remarked.

"Getting real tired...putting on those stupid things."

"What about the media?"

"Folks 'round here gonna protect me," he replied softly, edging toward Terry, so that the small cluster of people which passed by them in the corridor at that moment couldn't hear him.

"Oh?" Terry said, a little puzzled.

"Made a nice donation to the hospital fund. And when Carly recovers, gonna donate lots more."

"Oh?" Terry repeated, not certain this news pleased him.

"Anyway," Murdoch stated. "She's registered in your name."

"Does the hospital know you're her father?"

"We didn't get into that."

"But they know I lied," Terry responded, definitely less pleased now.

"*Lied*.... Don't know I like that word. Covered *someone's* ass sounds better."

"Speaking of Carly..." Terry said abruptly. "How is she?"

"Come see for yourself."

Murdoch led him into her room. Walking toward her as she slept, Terry observed no difference. But then she stirred, for the first time at the hospital in his presence. He could see she wasn't nearly as pale as on the previous occasions. Then she opened her eyes and smiled.

"Hi, Dad," she said softly.

"Hi, honey."

"Who's this man?"

Murdoch didn't answer. Carly looked closely at Terry. He thought he detected a flicker of recognition in her gaze. Hoping to avoid any embarrassment over her possibly recalling their meeting on the streets of Hollywood, he decided to volunteer an identity.

"I'm your Uncle Terry," he told her.

"Uncle Terry?" she replied quickly. "Dad, I don't have an Uncle Terry."

"Yes you do," Murdoch said, winking at Terry. "Kind of a long lost relative."

"You don't believe us?" Terry offered. "Just check the hospital records."

That seemed to satisfy her. Or maybe she was just too tired to question further. In fact, she soon fell back asleep. Terry glanced at Murdoch, who winked again.

"Well, Uncle Terry," he chuckled. "You can see your niece is getting better."

"You check with the doctors...? I mean...besides all that donation stuff."

"They say she's out of the woods."

Murdoch beamed as he spoke. Once more Terry was cognizant of how happy he appeared. As though perhaps he'd turned some kind of corner in his life. Or, more likely, he was simply relieved that his daughter was improving.

"Remember the woman who came here the other day?" Terry asked him. "Lauren..."

"Sure."

"She knew Carly from Texas."

"That so..."

"She's great with kids..."

Murdoch didn't reply.

"Might be good idea...you let her visit Carly again."

"Sure, any time. Just let me know so I can be here."

"Might be better," Terry said carefully, "you not be here."

"We can trust her?"

"We can trust her," Terry answered.

Murdoch nodded, apparently approving. As Carly continued sleeping, they just stood there silently. Eventually, Terry edged toward the door to leave.

"Oh...Uncle Terry," Murdoch grinned.

"Yes?"

"Thanks again for saving my ass."

"Ditto," Terry replied, smiling for the first time since he'd gotten there.

CHAPTER TWENTY

"The good news," Rick said, addressing the entire team, "is that none of you got traded. Our whole team's intact."

It was the day following the trade deadline. All the players, wearing their uniforms, ready to take the field, sat or stood in the home locker room at Oakland Stadium. Glancing around the room, Terry saw looks of relief on virtually everyone's face.

"The bad news," Rick continued, "is that Texas picked up a couple pitchers from Pittsburgh. And New York got Foster from Cincinnati for their weakness at third."

A few groans wafted about the room.

"But you know something..." Rick added. "I don't care. The fact those clubs made deals and we didn't doesn't bother me. After thinking it over, I'm glad we didn't bring in anyone new. You guys got us where we are, and you should have every opportunity to finish the job yourselves."

Terry noticed several of his teammates nodding as Rick, undoubtedly for effect, paused briefly.

"Maybe I'm old school," he went on, "but it just doesn't seem right to change horses in midstream. Bring in new players like Texas and New York. It almost seems like cheating.

"And anyway, Texas and New York can spend all the money they want...buy half a dozen players each, but just remember this, money doesn't buy chemistry."

Terry had never played organized football. But if he had, he was sure he wouldn't have heard a better pep talk.

"I don't believe it," Carly exclaimed, breaking into a wide grin.

Lauren grinned too. Before sitting down on a chair beside the bed, she reached for Carly's hand and held it. Terry, standing in the background a few feet away, saw how much better Carly looked. Very pretty and surprisingly alert. As he remembered her from that night in Hollywood. And, for the first time in his company, she was sitting up in bed, pillows propped against her back.

"Dad said someone from Texas might visit...I was hoping it was you."

Carly smiled as she spoke. But her expression quickly changed. In fact, she began to cry.

"I wish you didn't have to see me like this," she said.

"Me too," Lauren answered, touching Carly's face with her free hand.

"I wish I'd stayed after the baby was born."

"Don't worry about that now."

"I wish I'd stayed to see him."

"Maybe it's better you didn't."

"Does he have a good home?"

"I'm sure..."

From his vantage point, Terry could tell Carly had stopped crying. And that she and Lauren still held hands. He considered breaking his silence by asking Carly how she was feeling, but decided not to interrupt.

"Is there any way you could check on him?" Carly inquired of Lauren. "Just to be sure he's okay."

"I could try..."

"Thanks."

"You've got to stop running, Carly."

"I know..."

They chatted a while longer. Until it became apparent Carly was getting tired. Lauren got up from the chair and kissed her on the cheek.

"I'll keep in touch," she said.

"Promise?"

"Yes..."

"Good bye, Uncle Terry," Carly said softly.

"Good bye, Carly."

After leaving the room, Terry and Lauren had to sidestep a patient being wheeled down the corridor on a gurney. At the hospital lobby, Terry instinctively looked for her children, but then remembered she'd informed him, on the way to Carly's room, that she hadn't brought them today. He offered to accompany her to her car. When they exited the building, heading toward the parking structure, they were greeted by a strong wind.

"You have a nice way with her," he said. "She trusts you."

"Didn't seem to matter," she answered solemnly. "Didn't stop her running away."

"Still," he said after a pause. "She's a nice kid."

"She's a sweetheart.... That's what makes this so heartbreaking."

"Maybe it's not too late."

She didn't reply. He was also silent, partly because he had no more to say on the topic, and partly because the wind had blown something in his left eye. They reached the entrance to the parking structure, a two story covered edifice, and took a stairway up one flight.

"Sorry the kids didn't come today," he said.

"They're with my brother."

"Their uncle?"

"Yes, Terry," she winked. "My brother is their uncle."

He tried laughter to mask his embarrassment at being unable to master what was clearly a difficult concept for him. This whole "uncle" thing. A person can have more than one. A brother is automatically an uncle to his sister's children.

She attempted to ease his discomfort, or possibly change the subject, by handing him a cotton handkerchief for the windblown particle still in his eye, which he'd been rubbing intermittently with his fingers for the last minute or two.

"Their uncle..." he said slowly, careful not to utter anything else foolish. "He close to the kids?"

"Not as close as I'd like. He's a doctor and doesn't have much time."

"Married?"

"Divorced...five or six years."

"Any other relatives living here?" he asked, dabbing his eye with the handkerchief.

"No, I've kind of gotten away from family," she said. "The few still alive."

She pointed to her car up ahead, a yellow compact. They had to stop as another car, going too fast for a parking lot, whizzed by. The car belched black smoke, and they waited for the air to clear before resuming.

"Quite a coincidence that you should know Carly," he commented.

"Not so much as you'd think. In my prime I worked with hundreds of kids at a time."

"In your prime...?" he interjected a bit flirtatiously. "You don't look like you're past your prime to me."

She shrugged and appeared a little uncomfortable.

"Not like some broken down relief pitcher," he continued, flexing his right arm and presenting a pained expression, as though the arm hurt.

"Wish we could talk right now," she said, looking no less uncomfortable and glancing at her watch. "But I don't have time."

They reached her car. After unlocking the door, she looked up at him briefly. He felt a sudden impulse to kiss her. Right there in the parking lot, in broad daylight. Of course, he knew she would refuse. But he tried anyway. Surprisingly, she let him. And even kissed him back. In fact, he sensed she didn't want to stop.

"Stay a while," he coaxed, once they finally drew apart.

"No," she sighed. "I can't."

"Gotta go get the kids?"

"Sound instincts," she smiled. "Besides an uncle, you might make a good mother."

They both laughed. As she drove off, he rubbed his left eye once more with her handkerchief.

Late that night in his bungalow, Terry had trouble sleeping. Like that night nearly three months ago just prior to discovering Murdoch in trouble. Again, like then, he had the feeling too much was happening in his life, that things were a little out of control.

There were the relationships with all four Rileys and with Murdoch and Carly. With Rick. There was the pennant race. Plus the fact that earlier in the evening he'd recorded his twenty-second straight save, and been invited to appear afterward on postgame television.

"You're being mentioned," announcer Paul Furay had informed him, "as a leading candidate for rookie of the year."

Terry hadn't answered. Fortunately. Probably what he would have said was, if he won the award, he'd no doubt be the oldest recipient in history.

But now, as he tossed and turned in bed, unable to sleep, his thoughts centered on one thing. The kiss. What did it mean? Had he and Lauren reached a new plateau? Had she finally revealed her true feelings? Would he be seeing more of her? With and without the children.

Until then, all he'd really had the opportunity to do was admire her. The way she conducted herself. The knowledge and understanding she displayed with kids, especially problem children. The way she'd raised her own children, essentially alone and in the face of catastrophe with the sudden death of her husband.

Lying there in his bungalow, he knew he could no longer be satisfied just admiring her. Plain and simple, he wanted her. All of her.

The kiss had made that unmistakably clear.

Chapter Twenty-One

"Dad, when can I get out of here?" Carly asked the next morning.

"The doctor doesn't want you going yet, honey."

"Why not...? I'm feeling much better."

"There's no hurry."

"But I've been here more than a week," she debated, sitting up in bed.

"He's giving you medication," he said carefully. "To help withdrawal."

"Withdrawal...? Sounds like detox."

"I think that's what he has in mind. He says there's a good program right here at the hospital."

"But that's not what I have in mind," she answered sharply.

"I think you should listen to him."

"I listened to *you* back when we made our deal."

"I know honey. I'm just telling you what he said."

"I'm more interested in what *you* said and us keeping *our* deal."

"Our deal almost killed you," he replied softly.

His comment apparently registered, or maybe she paused because she wasn't feeling quite as strong as she thought. In either case, she lay back and closed her eyes, as if trying to sleep. Then she reopened them and looked up at Murdoch, standing beside the bed.

"Dad, I have something to tell you."

"What, honey?"

"It's about Texas."

"Texas?"

But she paused again, once more closing her eyes. This time Murdoch was nearly certain she'd fallen asleep, since her breathing grew heavy. Her eyes opened though, and he noticed tears in them. Also, that her expression had become very serious, reflective.

"I had a baby in Texas," she said.

He didn't reply.

"I had to give him up," she continued. "No money. No place for us to live."

"What about drugs?"

"That was a problem too."

Murdoch suddenly realized the extent of what his daughter had endured during the three years since he left her and her mother. He reached down and put his arms around her. He held her for several minutes, her initial tears turning into very audible sobs.

"Could you meet me at the hospital tomorrow?" Lauren asked Terry over the phone late that night.

"Sure."

"And maybe have lunch afterward..."

"Sure," he said, becoming curious.

"Around eleven?"

"Fine. Bringing the kids?"

"No. I'll get a sitter."

After hanging up, Terry had trouble getting back into the book he'd been reading. This was all new—her phoning, suggesting they meet, making a date for lunch, arranging a sitter for the kids. What did she have in mind?

Was this indication things were heading in the direction he hoped?

There were two outs and two on in the bottom of the ninth. Oakland trailed Baltimore 4-3 in what had been a very intense night game. Catcher Chris Bailey, a righty and number nine man in the batting order, was the scheduled hitter. He'd been in a slump and was 0 for 3 tonight. Rick decided to use a pinch hitter.

Clancy Adams was his choice. He strode determinedly to the plate. Unfortunately, he was also right handed, and had to face Jose Tartabull, Baltimore's talented closer, a right hander himself.

Rick had meant what he'd told his players about being happy with the guys they had. About not changing horses in midstream. About team chemistry. And yet, unless he held back one of his starters, he didn't have a single left handed pinch hitter. In this spot, against Tartabull, with the game on the line, he would've loved to have had a lefty.

Adams dug into the box. The Oakland runners led off first and second. Tartabull fired his first pitch, a tough slider over the outside corner at the knees. Adams took it for strike one.

Rick could bemoan Texas and New York picking up new players to strengthen weaknesses. But, he had to laugh. Each team had lost their last four games. Oakland now trailed them both by a mere game and a half.

Tartabull's next pitch was a curve that hung a little as it caught the outside corner. Rick couldn't avoid envisioning a left hander connecting and driving the pitch into right center for a game-ending two run double. The best Adams could do was foul the ball lazily over the Baltimore first base dugout, into the stands. Strike two.

Despite his desiring a lefty, there was no way Rick would want the front office to try and buy a championship. In recent years, while coaching in the minors, he'd seen many major league teams make the attempt and fail miserably, mortgaging their futures in the process. He resented the corporate mentality now seemingly dominating the sport. The concept that possessing resources to acquire the best players was far more important than some basic components of the historical American dream—working hard, developing talent, building from within. Baseball, once so intertwined with that dream, now appeared to be more its antithesis. In the process—as the elderly man Rick met on his San Diego flight had asserted—losing its purity and magic, the aspects Rick so admired. And with them, its very heart and soul.

Tartabull fired his next pitch. It was another curve, outside and in the dirt. Adams took a feeble half swing, and missed. Strike three, three outs, game over.

Rick headed sadly for the locker room. They'd have another game tomorrow night.

"Any news about the baby?" Carly asked, sitting up in bed.

"He's doing fine," Lauren reported.

"Good home?"

"Very..."

"In Texas?"

Lauren nodded. So did Carly, but rather glumly. In fact, Terry, standing in the background like during the previous occasion here at the hospital, could see she wasn't very happy. Not that it affected her appearance. Dressed in a new pink bathrobe Murdoch had evidently bought her, she looked even more alert than last time. When he and Lauren had entered the room, she'd even gotten out of bed and hugged them both.

"Any chance I could go see him?" she asked Lauren. "Once I get out of here."

"Not a good idea..."

"But I'm his mother."

"You gave up all rights."

"What would I have to do to get them back?"

"Are you asking for my help?" Lauren answered.

"Yes."

"There's only one way."

"What?"

"I think you know..."

"Go through a drug program," Carly petulantly replied, scowling.

"Correct."

"I can't."

"You can't...? Or you won't...?"

Carly didn't respond.

"I think you're being silly," Lauren said. "You've got your whole life ahead."

There was silence. Clearly they had reached an impasse. Terry suspected they'd had this same confrontation before. No doubt with the same result.

"A few days ago," Lauren said, "I told you I'd keep in touch, but I won't be able to much longer..."

"Because of me," Carly responded angrily. "Because I won't enter detox."

"No Carly...because of me."

"What do you mean *because* of you?"

"Because..." Lauren said, obviously uncomfortable, glancing briefly at Terry. "Because...because I'm sick."

"Sick? What do you mean...sick?"

"Just as I said. I'm sick."

"But you're going to get better," Carly said, clearly alarmed.

"No Carly. According to the doctors... I'm not."

"You're not going to...to..."

"It doesn't look good..."

Lauren's voice tailed off and silence ensued. The horrified look on Carly's face perfectly expressed Terry's feelings. When tears ran down her cheeks, he also felt like crying. He kept glancing at Lauren, hoping for some indication this was all a dreadful mistake. Her somber expression told him it wasn't.

"So you see," Lauren said, "why I think you're being silly. You've got your whole life ahead, so don't throw it away."

Another silence. Murdoch picked that moment to pop into the room, transferring attention to himself. Unquestionably, very much to the others' relief.

"We'll leave you with your dad now," Lauren said, then gave Carly a hug.

"Will you come back?" Carly asked. "I mean...as long as you're able."

"Yes," Lauren responded. "I'll come back."

After saying good bye to Murdoch and Carly, Terry followed Lauren out of the room. As they walked down the corridor, numerous questions ran through his mind. He didn't know where to begin, and was actually thankful she spoke first.

"Let's not say anything now. Let's just go find a nice place to talk."

They took his rental car. Neither of them uttered more than half a dozen words until they arrived at the restaurant he picked out a little more than an hour ago on his way to the hospital. For the lunch date she'd called him about.

CHAPTER TWENTY-TWO

"I'm so sorry," Lauren began. "I should have told you way before this... In private."

Terry could see she was fighting back tears. Instead of feeling like crying himself, as he had at the hospital, he simply felt numb. Too numb to even say something at that moment.

"I intended to tell you after we saw Carly," Lauren resumed. "But it just kind of slipped out back there."

"Cancer?" he barely mumbled.

"I've got lupus. I've had it for years. It didn't get bad, though, until...until after the car accident. They think the stress of everything set it off."

"And it's life threatening?" he managed.

"I'm afraid it is. Most people with lupus survive, but I'm subject to blood clots. I've already had three bad episodes."

He could only shake his head.

"They've warned me," she continued grimly. "Another could be..."

He shook his head again. Their waiter came over to take their order. Understandably, neither of them were hungry right then, however, so they asked him to come back.

The restaurant he had selected was unique. It was a mixture of American diner with a retro look, yet had a definite European flavor featuring paintings of famous locales like the Eiffel Tower and the Danube.

"I almost told you in the parking lot the other day," she said.

"You mean when stupid me joked about you being in your prime," he replied glumly. "I'm sorry... I didn't know."

"Don't apologize. You *didn't* know."

"So this is what you meant weeks ago at your place when you said there were some things I didn't know."

"Yes," she answered softly. "I should have told you right then."

"Why didn't you?" he asked just as softly.

"I guess because I didn't know you well enough. I wasn't sure...how I felt."

"About me?"

She nodded.

"Why did you wait *this* long?" he asked her gently.

"I'm not sure.... Maybe because of the kids. I didn't want to spoil your relationship with them. With Billy. He's doing so much better."

"You thought I'd stop seeing all of you if I knew? Run away like Carly."

"Something like that," she replied somberly.

He could see she was fighting back tears again. He reached across the table and touched her arm.

"Speaking of the kids," he said. "Any plans?"

"You mean...if...?"

He nodded solemnly.

"I don't know," she shrugged. "I was hoping my brother would take more interest, but he's got his own life. And, they're not so crazy about him either."

"Is he why you moved here?"

"Yes...his being a doctor. With access to more current treatments than I could get in Texas."

"Has he helped?"

"He's tried," she sounded grim. "But short of a cure..."

"There's no chance...this whole thing's not some terrible mistake?"

"No. No chance."

"You look pretty healthy to me," he said, smiling weakly while grasping for any particle of hope.

"I've been lucky so far. I've shown very few external symptoms, other than losing some weight. Which you might have noticed."

Indeed he had. The fact that she was slender, at any rate, which he'd assumed was a natural characteristic, not a symptom of some life-threatening condition.

He still had other questions. Things like medications and specific treatments. But he restrained himself. Really, what was the point at this particular time? The waiter came over for their order again, reminding him there was still lunch to try and salvage. Regardless of any lack of appetite either or both of them had.

They did manage to get through the meal, however, primarily by chatting about the kids.

After lunch, he took her to her car, which like last time, was parked in the hospital lot. He parked his car and walked with her to hers. Once she unlocked her door, he kissed her tentatively. She pulled away almost immediately.

"You sure you want to do this?" she asked, sounding drained.

He looked at her briefly. Then he kissed her passionately, holding her very close. This time she responded, throwing her arms around him too.

Terry's consecutive save streak ended that night. The explanation was simple—once the news about Lauren sunk in completely, he couldn't concentrate. He wandered around aimlessly the rest of the day. He couldn't eat, he couldn't read, he couldn't nap, and he even had trouble finding his way to the ball park.

When he entered the game to begin the ninth, Oakland led Kansas City 5-3. He faced six batters before Rick mercifully removed him. His problem was control of his pitches—either he wasn't able to locate the strike zone, or he sent them right down the middle. Three walks and three doubles put Kansas City ahead 7-5, a lead they never relinquished.

It was Terry's first major league loss.

"I've made a decision," Carly greeted Murdoch after he entered her hospital room.

"What, honey?"

"Spoke to the doctor a few minutes ago."

"Yes?"

"I begin the drug program here tomorrow."

Murdoch was astounded. Here he'd been agonizing over the road trip about to begin (the hospital was his final stop before the airport, in fact). Like before the last trip, to New York, he'd even considered not going. Maybe try to arrange a personal leave so he could keep an eye on her. Or, at the very least, fly back once or twice during the trip. But now, unexpectedly, she provides the perfect solution at the ideal time. Where she would remain here, under close supervision. Where, he knew from personal experience with her mother's drug programs, his presence was neither required nor even welcomed.

'What made you decide, honey?"

"Lauren."

"Lauren?"

"Yes," she answered. "Lauren."

He didn't reply.

"If she can show all the courage she's showing in her situation," she continued, "least I can do is show a little in mine."

Murdoch gazed at her questioningly, so she elaborated. She told him how Lauren had helped her during the pregnancy, guiding her through that difficult period. How she, Carly, had run away after the baby was born. How she'd interpreted Lauren's recent reentry into her life as a definite omen. Then, lastly, Carly disclosed Lauren's current crisis.

"If I don't get myself straightened out," she declared, "I've wasted everything she's done for me."

As when she first told him of the baby, Murdoch put his arms around his daughter and held her several minutes. This time it was his eyes, not hers, which started to moisten.

Terry began a new streak. Unfortunately, this one was negative. For the second consecutive time, he suffered a blown save. And this performance was no better than the prior.

It should have been easy. Oakland led 7-3 in the bottom of the ninth in Seattle. At the same stadium where he'd gotten his first save almost three months ago. The same sounds of a train whistle blowing greeted his entry into the game from the bullpen. The same late-night foggy condition existed as he stood on the mound with two on and two out. His first pitch hit the first batter, loading the bases. The next batter hit the next pitch to deep left field. This time Murdoch wasn't able to catch it, not when it landed halfway up the bleachers for a game-tying grand slam.

There was some good news. Franks, whom Rick summoned to replace Terry, got the final out of the ninth, and then pitched a scoreless bottom of the tenth. And Murdoch hit a two-run double in the top of the inning, propelling Oakland to a 9-7 win.

"Make me a promise..." Lauren said to Terry, the two of them sitting with Karen and Tammy in the grandstand at Billy's Little League park.

"Sure..."

"No sympathy."

He nodded.

"I don't want you feeling sorry for me," she emphasized. "*Or* for the kids."

"I promise. No sympathy."

She didn't reply, but appeared satisfied with his response.

"Truth is," he grinned, attempting to lighten a tense moment, "the way I've pitched lately, I'm the one that might ask for sympathy."

She smiled. His gaze turned to Billy out on the mound. The game was in the first inning and the boy had started well, striking out the first two hitters. It seemed to Terry that the batters were having trouble seeing Billy's deliveries in the early evening twilight, since the sun had disappeared and it wasn't dark enough yet for the park lights to provide much illumination.

Terry had phoned Lauren from Seattle near the end of the series there, and she informed him Billy's team, "The Dodgers," was playing in the league championship game tonight, and Billy was pitching. Since today was an off day for Oakland and the next game wasn't until tomorrow night in Texas, Terry had gotten permission from Rick to fly to San Francisco this morning, then on to Texas later tonight.

"Feeling okay?" he asked Lauren after Billy fired a strike to the next hitter.

"Make me another promise..."

"Sure..."

"No hanging on every sniffle."

"Sure," he replied brusquely, a bit hurt.

"Sorry," she said, touching his hand. "Guess I'm a little worried. I saw the doctor this morning..."

She paused briefly. He wasn't sure whether it was for effect, or because Billy had thrown another strike.

"He told me I shouldn't get my hopes up," she continued. "That there are often cases like mine with very few symptoms, then practically overnight, the patient falls apart.... I don't want to fall apart."

He was aware of the tears in her eyes. But he also saw determination in them. Though several thoughts ran through his mind, he didn't verbalize them. Not that she would have been able to hear him right then, anyway. Billy had fired strike three for the third out, and spectators cheered. Karen and Tammy, both seated on the other side of Lauren from Terry, may have been the loudest, informing everyone within earshot that Billy was their big brother.

There were two outs in the bottom of the sixth, the last scheduled inning of the Little League championship game. The Dodgers led 1-0, on Billy's run-scoring triple. Terry could see tension in the expressions of most of the people sitting nearby. Tension certainly having to do with the score, but probably more a reflection of the fact that Billy, with only one batter left to retire, was pitching a no hitter.

He fired a strike. Spectators applauded. Terry felt tense himself, as if he were the one on the mound, not Billy. It was completely dark now, well past twilight, and the park lights were in full force, which should have enabled batters to see Billy's pitches much better than earlier. Something not indicated, though, by the last five batters, all strike out victims.

Strike two. One more and Billy would have his no hitter and The Dodgers the championship. He wound up and threw the next pitch. The batter swung and lifted a little pop fly beyond the mound. Terry gasped, fearful the ball would drop before any of the infielders could get to it.

But Billy, running back and reaching over his head and behind himself, snagged it in the webbing of his glove for the final out.

His teammates mobbed him, right there in the middle of the field, where he'd caught the ball. Terry, Lauren and the girls got up to join him, but sat back down following the introduction of an awards ceremony. In the next few minutes, Billy and all his teammates received individual trophies commemorating their championship. And Billy won a special plaque for being the league's most valuable player. On their way to the field, once the ceremony was over, Terry couldn't help beaming.

"Congratulations," he said to Billy, shaking his hand.

"Thanks, Terry," Billy replied, showing hardly any of his usual shyness. "For all your help."

"I hope just a little of your talent rubs off on me," Terry grinned, still gripping Billy's hand.

CHAPTER TWENTY-THREE

Murdoch rarely exchanged words with his teammates on the road. Or at home either, for that matter. Clearly he preferred his own company. Therefore, Terry was surprised when, during pregame batting practice in Texas, Murdoch approached him as he stood near the bullpen in left field.

"Thought you might be interested," Murdoch began. "Carly's doing good."

"I was wondering..."

"Your friend's been a solid influence."

"Lauren?"

"Yes, Lauren," Murdoch replied. "Carly told me about her...situation. Sorry to hear."

"Thanks."

"She got Carly to begin a drug program," Murdoch said.

Terry was surprised again, recalling Carly's staunch opposition. Murdoch told him she now resided in a very plain dormitory-style facility at one end of the hospital. And, that although her first few days at the program hadn't been easy, she was determined to finish.

"You able to call her?" Terry asked.

"Any night between seven and ten."

"What about visiting?"

"By appointment only. With the approval of the program administrator."

A fly ball from batting practice landed nearby and Terry retrieved it, tossing it back toward the infield.

"Oh...almost forgot," Murdoch chuckled. "She asked about her Uncle Terry."

"What you say?"

"That he looks kinda lost and could use some help, and might take him out for dinner."

"That an invitation?" Terry asked, surprised once more.

"That's an invitation," Murdoch answered.

*****

Evidently none of Billy's pitching talent rubbed off on Terry. Not later that night in Texas, anyway. No doubt his just being in Texas had plenty to do with it. His unpleasant memories here before the trade. The possibility that, based on recent performance, he could wind up here again—back in the minor leagues. And naturally, just to reinforce all this, it was a very hot August night.

Trudging off the mound after blowing his third consecutive save, he took no consolation from the fact this outing was actually a slight improvement over the two previous. In those, he failed to retire a single batter. All eight men reached base safely. Tonight, of the four batters he faced, one at least did not reach base. The one who hit a 350 foot line out to center field. A sacrifice fly that drove in the winning run.

"Maybe someone else should be closing," Terry told Rick.

"You're the closer."

"I haven't been doing the job."

"You're the closer," Rick repeated.

The two men stood silently a moment, in the visiting manager's office at Chicago Stadium, half an hour before their game. Terry had purposely waited until they left Texas to confer with him, almost certain nothing positive could ever occur there. Also, he hoped Rick's mood would improve with a change in scene, since Oakland had just lost three straight in Texas, dropping them five games behind in their division, three and a half for the wild card.

"Spot anything I'm doing wrong?" Terry asked.

"No, except your concentration."

The two men looked at each other. Terry could tell Rick wasn't happy. Why should he be? His team was in a losing streak. And his closer had lost his concentration.

"Can't expect to be the closer," Terry said grimly, "if I'm not doing the job."

"You've done the job," Rick responded emphatically. "Even you don't get another save the rest of the season."

Terry didn't reply.

"Where would we be without you? You've taken the pressure off the other pitchers. Starters know all they have to do is throw six, seven good innings. And the other relievers—they know they get the game to you, we got a solid chance to win."

"Not lately."

"Okay...so you had a couple bad outings. But that doesn't change things. Everyone still thinks the same way. They get the game to you, you're gonna finish it."

Terry was silent.

"Long as I'm the manager," Rick declared, "you're the closer."

When he walked onto the Chicago Stadium field ten minutes later, Terry felt much better. His manager had confidence in him. Maybe that would make a difference in his next performance.

It didn't. Not that the Chicago batters had anything to do with it. No, for all intents, Oakland could just as easily been playing in Detroit or Cleveland or New York. Simply put, the Chicago batters never had a chance to hit. Before Rick removed him from the game, Terry walked the only three he faced. On twelve straight pitches out of the strike zone.

Franks, his replacement, also failed this time. He inherited a 6-3 lead, albeit with the bases loaded, thanks to Terry. A double and two singles later, Oakland had lost 7-6.

Afterward, Terry remained in the dugout, sitting by himself. For some reason he remembered his appearance on postgame television, when the announcer mentioned the rookie of the year award. What a joke! What a difference a couple of weeks could make! At this rate, he might not last the season, whether Rick believed in him or not.

One thing for certain, no way the award would be given to someone who finished the season back in the minor leagues.

"Do the kids know?" Terry asked Lauren.

"Yes," she answered softly.

Silence followed, except for the mingled sounds of baseball and music coming from the children's rooms. The road trip had finally ended, and they both were sitting in their regular place, on her living room couch. He touched her forearm as he spoke again.

"What do they know?"

"That there are times when I don't feel well. That I might be going to the hospital. That I might not be coming home."

His only response was a shake of his head. How could things have gone so bad so quickly? His pitching career in the tank. And far worse, the news about her.

"I told them," she went on with resignation in her voice, "that sooner or later it happens to everyone."

"They understand?"

"I think so. One consolation, unlike with their father, with me they will at least have had some warning."

"I don't think that's much consolation," he said sadly.

She nodded.

"What about Tammy?" he asked. "She's a little young to make sense of all this."

"I told her that after the hospital maybe I'd go off to some strange faraway land."

It was his turn to nod.

"Of course," she added, smiling faintly, "she wanted to go with me to the faraway land."

He smiled also. He decided to discontinue his probing, especially since the evening, at least until now, had gone so well.

The circus was in town. Much earlier, they had taken the children. Surprisingly, Karen enjoyed it the most. For some reason, she'd felt instant affinity with the trapeze artists. Following the performance, with Terry's help, she'd even gotten autographs from them.

After the circus, they had stopped for hamburgers. Then for ice cream at a little parlor. Back at the house, Terry had willingly provided equal time between Billy's room and the girls', listening first to baseball, then to music.

"I didn't realize Karen was drawn to danger," he told Lauren, recalling her attraction to the trapeze artists.

"I don't think she is. She just likes people who are."

"I guess we have that in common."

But his last words diminished in volume. For his interest in conversation was declining in proportion to his increase in interest in her, sitting beside him. Yes, she looked sad from their conversation and tired from their earlier activities, yet she still looked very pretty to him. As he gazed at her, he noticed her nose and her neck, and how feminine they appeared.

He touched her neck and gently drew her toward him. He hugged her. Then he kissed her. She responded, at least at first. As louder sounds came from the children's rooms, however, she pulled away.

"The kids..." she said. "I'm afraid this isn't the right time."

"*Time*, Lauren," he reacted strongly. "Who knows how much we have left?"

What happened next possibly could only be explained by all his recent frustrations. Her illness. Carly's problems. His own awful pitching. It certainly was far from his style to force himself on anyone.

But that's exactly what he did. He tried to kiss her again. And again. She kept pushing him away.

Finally she angrily got up off the couch. He angrily got up too, and headed for the door. She made no attempt to walk him there, nor did either of them speak a single word. He didn't even say good bye to the kids.

As he closed the door behind himself, once more he heard the mingled sounds of baseball and music coming from their rooms.

Terry spent most of the next day brooding about his behavior at Lauren's. Fortunately, there was a game that night, so he could get his mind off things for a while. Fortunately, he didn't have to pitch, so he couldn't add to his streak of ineffectiveness. Unfortunately, Oakland lost again, a 9-2 thrashing at the hands of Toronto.

After the game, he drove home with Collie Quinn, who mentioned that he'd lined up a couple of women. One was for him, Collie, and the other was for Jack O'Rourke. O'Rourke, though, had to stay and get treatment on a temperamental hamstring. Would he, Terry, like to substitute? In his dismal mental state, Terry reluctantly accepted.

"You won't be sorry," Collie said. "She's a knockout."

"Why don't *you* take her then?"

"Wish I could. But I'd lose my source."

"Your source your girl?" Terry asked.

"You got it."

Collie turned out right, Terry's woman *was* a knockout. She was in her mid-twenties, blonde, busty and had long alluring legs. The last item was evident while she and her partner, a brunette who was not nearly as attractive, did a sort of striptease in the middle of Collie's bedroom floor.

Loud music was playing. Terry and Collie each sat on a bed on opposite sides of the room. Terry watched Collie as he definitely watched *his* girl much more than he watched his own. The women were tossing clothing everywhere. With each article, Terry was growing more depressed as he kept flashing back to last night with Lauren.

"You're absolutely in the big leagues now, Terry," Collie shouted gleefully across the room. His unkempt long red hair flowed as he bent down to snatch a couple of female clothing items.

The women finished their dance. Nearly in a state of undress, they scurried into a bathroom. Terry motioned for Collie to turn down the music. He obliged.

"Wish we could trade, man," Collie said, his tongue practically hanging out. "Love that blonde."

"I've got a better idea."

"What?"

"You can have them both," Terry spoke firmly while getting up off the bed and heading for the door.

"Hey man, where you goin'?"

"To my place."

"Want me to send the blonde over?"

"No," Terry sounded even more definite.

"Hey man, what do I do with *two* women?"

"Same thing you'd do with one, except have *twice* the fun."

Terry opened the door and shut it firmly behind himself.

CHAPTER TWENTY-FOUR

"Back off!" Murdoch exclaimed. "No way! I'd go full speed ahead. On both counts."

"But I'm not getting anywhere with her, and I hurt the team every time I pitch."

The two of them were sitting across a corner table from each other in an expensive Italian restaurant with red and white cotton tablecloths and photographs of various locales in Italy on the walls. Terry had already informed Murdoch of the episode with Lauren, and his discussion with Rick about remaining the closer. Plus that, in both areas, he was inclined to retreat. Revelations that caused Murdoch's strong reaction.

"Let's start with baseball," Murdoch advised, aggressively digging his fork into a large plate of spaghetti.

"Okay," Terry replied, showing much less appetite for a ravioli dish.

"That first slump is key to staying in the big leagues. Guys who can't hang in there and fight their way through end up back in the minors."

Terry didn't reply. Instead he gazed between his ravioli and Murdoch.

"Same with Lauren," Murdoch continued. "You got to be patient and fight your way through."

"She acts like she doesn't want me," Terry replied sadly.

"She say that?"

"Not in so many words."

"I read her right," Murdoch said, about to ingest a huge forkful of spaghetti, "she's damn proud. Hates the idea of sympathy."

"You read her right."

"And you want to back off...?"

Terry shrugged.

"How'll she interpret that?"

Terry shrugged again.

"I'll tell you how. That you really don't care. That you're not willing to hang in and fight this thing through. And no question in my mind she's worth it."

Terry sensed that Murdoch was about to say more. That he was aware of things that he could reveal. But, he kept quiet at that point.

Meanwhile, Terry's only response was to poke at a piece of ravioli with his fork. He felt full, despite over half his dinner remaining. Murdoch quickly devoured the rest of his food, and then glanced at Terry's as if he intended to finish it too.

"I say you *escalate*," he declared, motioning for their waiter.

"Escalate?" Terry questioned. "How?"

"I'll leave that up to you."

Murdoch did end up eating most of the rest of Terry's meal. When their waiter came over, he requested a slice of apple pie with three scoops of ice cream, and seemed very disappointed when Terry declined to order dessert.

More than two weeks had passed since Lauren's awful disclosure. During that time, Terry had done only sporadic research on the subject of lupus. The very next day following the dinner with Murdoch, though, he spent the entire morning and early afternoon in the library, exploring the disease via books and computer.

What he found was lupus was an auto-immune disorder. Women were by far its most likely victims. It was both chronic and incurable.

There was some good news, however. The disease rarely caused death. It wasn't transmittable, and there was no evidence of it being hereditary.

These favorable items, though, were fearsomely offset by his findings on lupus and blood clots. Yes, they could be a problem. And yes, they could be fatal.

When he left the library, Terry certainly felt no better than when he got there.

Terry listened as the phone rang on the other end. He anticipated Lauren's voice. Instead, it was Karen who answered with a hello.

"Hi, Karen. Is your mama there?"

"Hi, Terry. She doesn't feel very well. She's taking a nap."

"I'll call back later."

"We're going out later," she quickly reported. "School starts tomorrow and Mama wants to buy us some supplies."

"How are you?"

"Fine."

"And Billy and Tammy?"

"Tammy's fine. She begins kindergarten. It's her first day of school ever."

"Nice. And Billy?"

"Sad."

"Sad?" he responded. "Why?"

"He asked Mama when you were coming over and she said you might not for a while. He asked her why, because he knows you're not on a road trip."

"What did she say?"

"She didn't answer him."

Terry didn't reply. He began to feel sad himself. Maybe he should speak to Billy. But then, that might only confuse things.

"Bye, Terry."

"Bye, Karen."

After hanging up, he pondered his next move.

Trying to analyze the team's recent decline, Rick sat in his office at Oakland Stadium, statistics for the first three weeks in August in front of him. Team batting average was below .220 for the period. On base percentage only .260. Slugging percentage barely .300. Earned run average over 6.00.

No wonder they'd managed only seven wins in twenty-two games played so far this month. And had fallen to six-and-a-half games behind Texas in the division and five behind New York for the wild card. How could he stop the bleeding?

He returned to the earned run average figures. And in particular to the bullpen. Their numbers were over 7.00 for the period. And, of course, that brought him to Terry.

Sure he'd told Terry he was the closer. But how long would front office stand for it? The blown saves and skyrocketing earned run average.

If things didn't get better soon, he might be forced to make a change. He might have to try someone else in the closer role.

CHAPTER TWENTY-FIVE

Terry parked his rental car—this one a blue and white mini-van—in front of the white house. Nothing to do now except wait. It was a cool overcast early-morning, and he zipped up his green windbreaker.

Fifteen minutes passed. Half an hour. He saw no sign of life in the house. What if things had changed? Or worse, he'd missed them entirely. He might just sit there all morning, waiting for something that wasn't going to happen.

Then finally Karen came out of the house. Followed by Tammy and Billy. Lauren appeared. The four of them headed for her yellow compact.

No one noticed him right away. Then, while getting into Lauren's car, Billy seemed to spot him. Billy waved and said something to Lauren. She headed toward Terry and, as he rolled down his window, he could see she looked puzzled.

"What are you doing here?" she asked.

"First day of school," he stated nonchalantly, as if the answer were obvious. "We can take my van."

Frowning, she shook her head and didn't reply. Was she simply surprised by his presence? Or was he not welcome?

"Tammy's first day of school ever," he chuckled. "Wouldn't miss it for the world."

She broke into a smile. It was beginning to mist and she looked up toward the sky. Then she shrugged.

"More room in my car," he said.

She shrugged again and waved the kids over. While they were coming, she returned to her car and got an umbrella. He smiled once they'd all gotten into his car.

"Do you know the way?" she asked.

"Checked it out before I came to the house," he winked at her.

The school was only a few blocks away. By the time they reached it, the mist had stopped. He parked near the front of the school. He and Lauren got out with the kids.

"Want us to walk with you to your class?" Lauren asked Tammy.

"No Mommy, I'm a big girl now."

He chuckled again. Lauren gave all three kids a hug and he patted them on the back. The kids left for the school together. Tammy stopped them after a few steps and they doubled back.

"Mommy," she said, "can Terry come over after school and listen to music and baseball?"

"We'll see, honey," Lauren grinned. "We'll see."

"He can't Tammy," Billy said. "He has a game."

Terry grinned too.

"I think," Terry said to Lauren as he pulled up in front of her house again, "we should do something we've never done before."

"What?" she asked, looking both dubious and puzzled.

"Go out on a Saturday night date. Just the two of us. No kids."

Again, she looked dubious and puzzled. Actually, he didn't know exactly *what* he had in mind. He merely sensed that they badly needed time together, just the two of them, in a relaxed environment.

"No kids," was all he would say, for the second time.

With that, he simply walked her to her front door, went back to his car, and drove off.

"Things going any better, honey," Murdoch said during what had become his regular evening conversation with Carly.

"They don't make it easy, Dad."

"That's part of the deal," he replied, recalling dialogue with Sheila while she was in drug rehab.

"They have tough rules, Dad. Won't bend them for anybody."

"It'll be over before you know it."

"Dad, do you know how Lauren is doing?"

"I'll check with Uncle Terry."

"I wonder if she knows any more about the baby."

"I'll try and find out," Murdoch spoke a little vaguely.

"Dad, they've got me looking at a lot of things."

"That's what they do."

"Dad?"

"Yes, honey?"

"I'm so sorry for all the grief I've caused."

He could tell she was close to crying, and was almost glad when she soon hung up.

CHAPTER TWENTY-SIX

"I hear they need a singer for the next song," Terry told Lauren, a mischievous smile on his face.

She looked at him strangely. They'd been on their "Saturday night date" for about an hour. The six-piece band, which had been on break, began to queue up for its next set. Terry glanced at them. Then, still smiling, he turned back to Lauren, sitting beside him at their table.

The music started. He watched her, able to tell from her expression that she recognized the song from the very first bars. "Fever" was playing.

"They need a singer," he coaxed, a grin replacing his smile.

"You're not serious," she objected.

"Of course I am. That's your song."

"I couldn't possibly," she looked a bit flustered. "It was so long ago."

"Well, then," he kept grinning, "the least you can do is dance with me."

"Okay," she sounded hesitant. "As long as you don't mind how rusty I'll be."

"As long as you don't mind," he quickly retorted, "how awful I dance."

The reason for his statement became evident right away. Once they reached the nearby dance floor, his movements were awkward at best. He was thankful she didn't laugh. Meanwhile, if she was rusty, he couldn't tell. She was graceful, a splendid dancer.

"Wish I could say I was just rusty," he uttered once they returned to their table.

"I suppose you arranged that," she said, ignoring his comment.

"Arranged what?" he asked, his expression as innocent as he could muster.

"That song."

He shrugged, doing his best to maintain innocence. Rather than look at her and risk a guilt-confirming chuckle or laugh, he watched the band, which was performing another number. From there, he gazed around the elegant nightclub. Situated atop a luxurious San Francisco Nob Hill hotel, it offered a spectacular view of the city spread out before them. Crystal chandeliers hung from a high ceiling above.

Finally, he turned back to her. She looked absolutely lovely in a lavender dress. It was the first time she'd worn a dress in his presence. Her earrings sparkled, and prompted him to notice her ears, which stuck out ever so slightly, in a very charming way. She seemed quite comfortable in her attire, unlike him. He'd worn brown, a sports coat and tie, and they both made him squirm occasionally because they fit too snugly.

"About the other night..." he said. "I want to apologize."

"Please don't."

"I was out of line."

"It was more me," she disagreed. "I just don't want us going places we shouldn't go...with my circumstances."

"I understand."

"Plus, there's something else..."

"What?" he asked.

"I'm afraid you're trying to take advantage of someone...in distress."

"I'd have given up long ago if that's what I was doing," he promptly countered.

She didn't reply. He glanced around the room again. Then he gazed at her once more.

"You look so...radiant," he said.

"Music always does that to me," she smiled.

"I'm still having trouble with the idea that you're...in distress. The way you look right now."

"We danced," was her simple explanation.

"You danced. I bumbled."

She laughed. He was discovering that he liked her laugh as much as he liked her smile. He was unable to keep from touching her arm.

"I'm sure," he went on cautiously, "you've done the research."

"On my condition? Of course I have."

"I mean this thing about...blood clots."

"Dozens of books and dozens of specialists."

"Are there things?" he asked, motioning toward the dance floor, "that they don't want you doing?"

"No. They want me living normally. Just so I take my medication."

"What kind?'

"Well," she replied after hesitating briefly, "if you want the gory details.... Blood thinners."

He paused to reflect. This information certainly concurred with his recent research. Unfortunately confirming what she had revealed weeks ago—that blood clots were the danger, and, no question, a potentially grave one.

"What about treatments?" he pressed on. "Or therapy?"

"None. Just weekly checkups with my doctor."

"Is he doing everything he can for you?"

"She. And yes, she is."

"If there's anything I can do..." he offered.

"Thanks."

The band continued playing. A waiter came over to take drink orders. Once he left, Terry braved touching her hand. She didn't move it, so he kept his hand there.

"Any more thought about the kids?" he asked.

"You mean for later on?"

"Yes."

"Yes, I'm working on something."

"Oh?"

"I've contacted a couple of adoption agencies."

"Adoption agencies!" he exclaimed, very surprised.

"Yes. All my years in social work, I've found some very selective ones."

"You mean you'd leave the kids with strangers!"

"Not with strangers," she corrected. "I'll interview very thoroughly."

He didn't reply right away. The waiter returned with their drinks. Still upset, Terry quickly sipped from his. He thought a minute before speaking again.

"Promise me something."

"What?"

"That you'll let me help interview," he said firmly. "Especially any final choice you're about to make."

"Okay..." she replied after a brief pause.

"Now," he spoke while glancing at the band. "How about another dance? I'll try to do better."

She grinned and got up. He held her hand and led her to the dance floor. The band started a new song.

He did do better this time. But only slightly.

"Would you like to come in?" Lauren asked Terry as they walked from his rental mini-van to her front door.

"Better not."

"Baseball tomorrow?"

"Yes. But that's not the reason."

"What is the reason?" she asked as they got to the door.

He hesitated. Wasn't this his opportunity? At last alone in the house with her, no kids to interrupt (she'd told him earlier in the evening they were spending the night with her brother).

"Well," he finally answered her, "Billy's probably told you how awful I've been pitching."

"He mentioned something."

"I've been terrible. Miserable."

"What's that have to do with coming inside?" she asked a little impatiently.

"Well," he risked, a slight chuckle in his voice, "I'm afraid you'll try to take advantage of someone...in distress."

She laughed heartily, so his risk had been worth it. It was also worth it to linger with her at her door, because she looked no less lovely than she had all evening. In fact, with the idea so firmly planted in his mind that he could be alone with her inside, she looked even lovelier. Wasn't he making a giant mistake?

"Are you sure?" she tested him some more.

"I'm sure," he held steadfast, then turned and began walking toward the van.

"Terry," she called after him.

"Yes?" he said, turning back toward her hopefully.

"I like you in a coat and tie."

"Thanks," he muttered.

After he drove off, the image of her standing beside him at her door stayed with him all the way home.

CHAPTER TWENTY-SEVEN

Terry began warming up. The afternoon sun was warm in the Oakland Stadium left field bullpen, and he knew it wouldn't take long. Oakland was batting in the bottom of the eighth with a 4-2 lead. Rick had already told him that he would pitch the ninth.

Conditions were almost perfect. The prevailing wind that Rick had often spoken of was blowing fiercely. Their opponent was Anaheim, a weak-hitting team. Plus, the lower end of their order was due up, the seven, eight and nine spots. Terry sensed that this was an easy save opportunity. But he also sensed that if he blew this one, very likely he would lose his job as the closer. No matter what Rick had told him.

"Good luck, Terry."

He promptly recognized the voice and turned. Karen, leaning over the wall to his right, waved to him. His memory could be forgiven because so much time had elapsed, but he was almost sure that the first time she had called to him, back in Texas, she was wearing the same blue dress she had on today. She pointed up into the grandstand a few rows. Lauren, Billy and Tammy were sitting there, and they also waved to him.

What a surprise. Although he'd talked to them all this very morning, Sunday, none of them mentioned coming to the game. If he'd known, he would have gladly left tickets for them. Maybe they'd decided to come at the last minute. Whether they were there for the entire game, or just part, he had no idea.

He focused on his warm-ups. On using the proper grip for the knuckler. On coming over the top. On keeping his wrist stiff. Oakland did not score in the eighth, so he had only the two-run lead when he entered the game.

As he faced the first Anaheim batter, a righty, he concentrated on the same items again—concentration, what had been missing from all his performances lately. He had no excuse today. Everything was in his favor. All the more since Lauren, Billy, Karen and Tammy were present.

Except the favorable wind soon betrayed him. Not because it adversely affected his knuckler. It didn't. No, the batter hit a twisting pop up down the right field line. First baseman Steiner could have easily caught it, but the wind blew it barely out of his reach. Runner on first, no outs, potential tying run, a lefty, coming to the plate.

The lefty hit a towering pop fly behind shortstop—what should have been an easy play for Oates, except the wind intervened again. This time, at the last instant, it swirled the ball over his head, and it fell untouched to the turf. Tying runs on, still no outs.

Terry turned and looked fitfully beyond the left field bullpen. Of course he couldn't spot Lauren and the kids from that distance, however he could imagine them watching. About to view another of his disasters? About to witness firsthand his removal from the closer role?

He gritted his teeth. No, he couldn't let that happen. He concentrated hard on doing everything right. He threw a perfect "diver" over the outside corner. The batter, another lefty, hit one more pop up. Again the wind played its demonic tricks, this time causing the ball to evade third baseman O'Rourke. But the infield fly rule came into effect, so the hitter was automatically out.

Another knuckler to the next batter, a righty. One more pop up. It was Collie Quinn's turn to tackle elements. He was no more successful than his infield mates, all of whom had squandered their chances. Again, the wind imposed, the ball twisting to earth right at his feet. Fortunately, once more, the infield fly rule prevailed. Two on, two outs.

Terry knew he couldn't succumb to these strange occurrences. He *had* to maintain concentration. One more batter to get. "Grip, over the top, stiff wrist," he reminded himself.

He started the next batter with two knucklers in the dirt. He threw a diver for a strike. The batter, another righty, fouled off the next pitch. If Terry hadn't been so focused, he would have marveled at the poetic aspects of the situation. Two balls, two strikes, two outs, two on, a two-run lead.

The hitter lofted a fly to left field. With the prior results, Terry almost couldn't look. If the wind played tricks on Murdoch, the ball might slip past him, all the way to the wall. Both runners would certainly score. Tying the game. Another blown save. Demotion to follow.

Murdoch ranged to his right. The ball danced and dipped in the wind, as if it was a knuckleball. Murdoch wobbled briefly, but he stayed with it. His glove was like a magnet, attracting the ball. It landed in the pocket and remained. The game was over, Oakland had won. Terry had his first save in about three weeks.

After the obligatory postgame handshakes, he jogged toward the left field bullpen, hoping Lauren and the kids were still there. On the way, he crossed paths with Murdoch, who had obviously disdained the handshakes. Murdoch motioned him to stop.

"Those infield cats," he chastised. "Can't catch nothin' if it hit 'em in the head. All they know is to party."

Terry laughed.

"You're a head case yourself," Murdoch went on. "All you gotta do, get 'em hit the ball to me. What I'm there for."

Terry laughed again. He continued on to the bullpen. Lauren and the kids *were* still there. Waiting for him? Or simply waiting for the crowd to dissipate, so they could get easily to her car?

"What a surprise," Terry greeted them as they stood above him, beyond the wall.

"Yay, Terry," Tammy shouted down at him.

"Should've let me know you were coming," he admonished.

"Didn't want to bother you," Lauren chuckled. "Heard you were...in distress."

He grinned.

"Wanted to give you a little inspiration," she added.

They had certainly done that. In more ways than one. Besides the game, just looking at her now, eyes gleaming down at him. Looking at the kids, obviously happy to be there.

He would have liked to have gone up in the grandstand right then, uniform and all, and given each of them a big hug.

"He's got his own life. And they're not so crazy about him, either."

Right after arriving at Lauren's house, Terry was able to verify the accuracy of her words, spoken weeks ago, about her brother Steven and the kids. It was the final night before the long homestand would end, and she wanted him to meet her brother prior to the next road trip.

He quickly noticed that, in Steven's presence, the kids were far more restrained than usual. Steven, a gruff chunky man with a beard, obviously many years older than Lauren, seemed very studious and devoted to his profession. He soon made his specialty known— dermatology—and spoke of it several times during the hour or so he was there.

Once Steven left, Terry happily fulfilled his regular stints in the children's rooms. Tammy was even more gleeful than normal as she showed him some pictures she'd painted at school. And Billy set a record for chattiness in Terry's company, contributing more than two dozen words to their conversation.

"He's becoming downright talkative," Terry beamed to Lauren afterward, the two of them at their customary stations on her living room couch. "I couldn't get a word in edgewise."

"I doubt that," she replied, shaking her head.

"He's doing good, that's the important thing," he commented. "All three kids are doing good. You've done a terrific job..."

She smiled that wonderful smile again. He loved being on her couch like this with her. He really didn't need anything else. Simply her nearness was enough.

And yet he couldn't keep from trying to kiss her. Even with the kids close by, making noise in their rooms. Even though she had rebuffed him less than two weeks ago.

Surprisingly, she let him. And let him kiss her again. And again. Finally, after the fourth kiss, he decided not to push his luck.

"I'm sorry," he said. "I can't help myself."

She touched his hand.

Terry followed up his nice "pop up" performance with another good outing, versus Anaheim again, on the final day of the homestand. Oakland won 3-1. Once more, Lauren and the kids attended, and sat in the same section behind the bullpen. This time, though, Terry knew they were coming, and arranged tickets.

His good pitching continued throughout the road trip. He converted four consecutive save opportunities. However, unfortunately, the team continued its spotty play, and got thrashed in all five of the other games on the trip.

The club arrived back in Oakland late Labor Day night, now trailing Texas by eight games, New York by six and a half. With only twenty-five games remaining in the regular season, it was crucial that they develop some positive momentum during the upcoming homestand, or forget any chance for the playoffs.

Fortunately, their schedule did include the two teams they were chasing. On the next road trip, they had three games in Texas. And at the end of this week, they had four with New York in Oakland.

A sweep of both series would no doubt propel them right back into contention.

CHAPTER TWENTY-EIGHT

"What do you think?" Lauren asked right after the middle-aged man and woman left the interview room at the adoption agency.

"I think they're nice," Terry answered.

"But would they make good parents?"

"They've already made good parents," he replied. "Two grown children of their own."

"I think that's the problem."

"What?" he questioned, a little puzzled.

"They're too old."

He didn't answer right away. The couple had been the fifth he and Lauren had interviewed that morning at the agency located on the ground floor of an old building in downtown San Francisco. All five couples had seemed solid candidates to him. All five had a fault or two, however, according to Lauren.

"I think," he finally said while they awaited the next interview, "that you're looking for perfection."

"They're my kids," she replied succinctly, as if no further explanation were needed.

"Well, I'm far from perfect too," he shrugged. "I guess that makes me as good a candidate as these other people."

"You're not a candidate," she said straightforwardly.

"Why not?" he was curious.

"You couldn't get court approval."

"Why not?" he was still curious.

"Very simple," she promptly answered. "You're not married."

"That's not a proposal, is it?" he winked.

She looked at him strangely. He winked again. She continued to look at him strangely.

"Another reason," she finally said. "You're a baseball player..."

"Bad role model? Better I be a doctor or a lawyer?"

"It's not that. It's all the time away from home."

He nodded, shrugged and frowned all at the same time. Probably his mixed responses were because he hadn't intended this discussion and didn't know how to react to it. In truth, he hadn't even given this particular subject much thought.

"And yet, I can't deny the kids like you," she spoke as if she was no more than thinking out loud. "No question about Billy and Tammy, and even Karen, who can be very picky. I watched her at the circus that time."

"So I am a candidate."

"No you're not," she said firmly. "You're not married."

"You're proposing again," he winked once more.

Walking toward the drug rehabilitation wing of the hospital, Terry felt quite content for a couple of reasons. Two hours ago he'd pitched a perfect ninth to close out a 6-4 afternoon victory over Minnesota, and Oakland had swept the series, giving them a perfect start to the homestand, before the important four game confrontation with New York.

Terry was here because Murdoch had invited him to a little ceremony. Carly had finished the drug program and tonight was her graduation. He reached a lobby outside the drug wing, and saw Murdoch and Carly standing together, chatting. When they noticed him, they both greeted him warmly, Carly with a hug. She wore a stylish tan pantsuit and Terry couldn't help comparing her appearance now with those first days in the hospital.

"Glad you could come, Uncle Terry," she spoke cheerily.

"Congratulations, Carly."

She grinned. So did Murdoch, possibly at her continuing to refer to Terry as her uncle. Carly excused herself to welcome another guest, a young man Terry assumed was a drug program participant.

"She looks great," Terry told Murdoch. "Wish you'd let me bring her a gift."

"No gifts," Murdoch emphasized, using the same words Terry recalled him using when inviting him. "Want nothing spoiling my little surprise."

Terry *was* surprised in the very next instant. Lauren, dressed in a dark slacks and blouse combination, entered the lobby with Billy, Karen and Tammy, also nicely attired. None of his recent conversations with them, the latest occurring just this morning, offered any inkling they'd be here.

"Why didn't you tell me they were coming?" he asked Murdoch. "That your little surprise?"

Murdoch's only response was a twinkle in his eye, and to quickly leave the lobby. Lauren and the children came over to Terry, taking turns hugging him.

When Carly spotted Lauren, she rushed right over, screaming excitedly. More hugs, these accompanied by tears. Tears of obvious joy.

Lauren introduced her to the kids. Another round of warm hugs.

"Why didn't you tell me you were coming?" Terry asked Lauren once Carly left them to greet other guests. "I didn't expect you."

"Shhh. It's all a surprise."

"On who?"

"You'll just have to wait and see," she smiled.

"How long?"

"Maybe five or ten minutes."

It actually took only five or ten seconds. Terry noticed Murdoch return to the lobby. He was carrying something in his arms. Something wrapped in a blanket. Was it a baby? No question, it was a baby. As Murdoch came closer, Terry could see a tiny brown face beneath the blanket.

Suddenly Carly gasped. And rushed to Murdoch. He handed her the baby. As she held it, Lauren went over and hugged her again.

"Ladies and gentlemen," Murdoch announced loudly. "I'd like to introduce Joshua, my grandson."

"So that was Murdoch's *little surprise*." Terry said to Lauren once she returned to him and the children.

She grinned.

"Guess you had plenty to do with it," he added.

"A *little*," she smiled, cleverly prolonging the theme.

"Why didn't you tell me?" he asked her for the second time that evening.

"Then it wouldn't have been a surprise," she answered teasingly. "Besides, there wasn't much to tell. The baby's adoption fell through. When I heard about it, I was able to arrange a court hearing. And we managed to persuade the judge to give Carly a trial period."

"Was Murdoch involved?"

"Very. He flew to Texas for the hearing, and convinced the judge that he would take complete financial responsibility."

Somewhat miffed all this had happened without his knowledge, Terry didn't reply.

"It turned out," she said, "that the judge was a baseball fan."

Murdoch came over as Terry, Lauren and the children stood in a corner of the lobby, sampling food they'd gathered from a buffet cart that had been wheeled in. Terry, still a bit vexed about being kept in the dark, wasn't very cordial to Murdoch. In fact, it was Lauren who introduced him to the children.

"Funny," Murdoch said. "Couple months ago, wasn't even sure I was a father. Now I'm a grandpa too."

Terry's vexation diminished substantially in the next few minutes. It almost always did when he was alone with Lauren. In this particular case, the two of them stood off by themselves in a corner of the lobby, simply watching her children interact with Carly and tiny Joshua.

"You see what I see?" Terry asked.

"Yes."

"Sure didn't take them long."

It certainly hadn't. The three kids had already bonded with Carly and the baby. In fact, Carly let them take turns holding him. And she couldn't keep from affectionately touching Billy, Karen and Tammy.

About an hour later, when Terry left the hospital with Lauren and the kids, he had completely forgotten his earlier dismay. He found Carly's actual graduation ceremony exhilarating. And the kids, Carly, and Joshua had continued their previous affinity.

True, he'd been a minor precipitator in the day's occurrences. No question Lauren, Murdoch, and Carly herself had played far more significant roles. But he had definitely been a participant. And that was more than enough for him.

When Terry entered the game, New York was batting in the top of the ninth. Oakland was leading 9-8, there were two outs, but the bases were loaded. Before the game, Rick had told Terry that he wouldn't be using him tonight (Terry had pitched in the last four games, all Oakland wins, and he had gotten the save in each).

Obviously, Rick had changed his mind. This game was too important. One more out and Oakland would sweep the four game series against New York and pull within two games of them for the wild card.

Terry finished his warm-ups and glanced around at all three baserunners. He flexed his right arm. It felt a little tired, like this *was* his fifth consecutive game. But all he needed was that one single out.

Jordan, the New York clean-up hitter, stepped into the left hand batters' box. Terry went through his "concentration" reminders. "Proper grip, over the top, stiff wrist." Bailey gave him the sign for the knuckler. Terry fired a good one, a diver, over the outside corner. Strike one.

He went through the same routine. After glancing at the runner edging off third, he chucked another knuckler. Jordan swung at this one and missed by a wide margin. Terry could tell by his look of frustration that Jordan knew he didn't have a chance. One more good one and the game would be over. Just one more strike.

Terry flexed his arm again. Bailey flashed the knuckleball sign. Terry fired. Another one that danced and dove. Jordan swung. A mighty swing. And missed by a mile. The plate umpire raised his right arm in what should have been a game-ending motion.

Except, Bailey missed the ball. It had moved so much that it avoided his glove on its path to the backstop.

Jordan ran to first and the runner from third scored easily. Tie game, 9-9.

A blown save. It was little consolation that Spencer, the next batter, lofted a fly ball to left field. And that Murdoch squeezed it for the final out of the inning. Terry could only shake his head as he trudged to the dugout. And anticipated Murdoch's chastising words, "Hey, head case all you gotta do is get 'em hit the ball to me."

But, after trotting in from the outfield, Murdoch seemed to have other things on his mind. He was the leadoff batter in the bottom of the ninth.

Heading to the plate, Murdoch hardly noticed the late-night cold. What he did notice, after being announced by the public address man, was that for the first time in years the cheers sounded louder than the boos. Not that it mattered. He simply noticed.

He wasn't likely to get anything to hit. Not from a New York pitching staff that had purposely walked him when he threatened DiMaggio's streak. Had purposely walked him throughout this series. Why would they change strategy now, in a game tied 9-9?

Not that he wouldn't like them to. Give him the chance to extract a little revenge for the cowardly way they'd protected the record. One swing of his bat could help settle that score.

He glared out toward the mound, at Carrasco, the New York closer. The same Carrasco who issued the final walk in New York, the walk that officially ended his hitting streak. Carrasco glared back at him, then fired the first pitch. A fastball directly at Murdoch's head. Same as his final pitch in New York. Dropping quickly to the ground, Murdoch heard the ball whistle just above his left temple. He got up and slowly dusted off his uniform, then glared at Carrasco again.

Once more, Carrasco glared back. Murdoch knew he would likely throw another head hunter. Certainly it was consistent with the theme. In fact, he might expect three more bean balls.

Carrasco surprised him. Or perhaps, simply missed his target. Regardless, he threw a fastball, letter high, over the inside corner. Murdoch swung hard. Connected. And sent a towering drive to left field that not only cleared the fence, but the high wall at the rear of the grandstand. A prodigious home run, later calculated at 562 feet.

Trotting around the bases, Murdoch didn't hear a single boo in the loud ovation.

Terry had blown the save in the top of the ninth, but he got the win. More importantly, so did Oakland. With less than three weeks left in the regular season, they now trailed New York by only two games.

CHAPTER TWENTY-NINE

"Terry, can we stop for pizza?"

"No, Tammy. I think we'd better get back and check on your mother."

Terry's answer seemed to satisfy her. He glanced in the rearview mirror of his car, a different mini-van than last time, and saw Billy and Karen, sitting next to Tammy in the backseat, nodding their agreement. The four of them were driving back from an outdoor concert in Golden Gate Park, San Francisco's diverse cultural complex and sprawling parkland about fifteen minutes from the Rileys. Lauren was to have gone also, but she declined at the last minute, claiming she might be coming down with a cold. Concerned it could be more, Terry had looked at her questioningly, but decided not to probe.

"Terry..." Karen said. "Billy wants to ask you something."

"Sure..."

"Go ahead, Billy," she spoke bossily.

"Well..." Billy began uncomfortably.

"Go ahead, Billy," Karen continued impatiently. "Ask him."

"Well...Terry...You're not..."

"Not what, Billy?" Terry asked softly.

"You're not...going to...go away?"

"You mean...like your father did?"

"Yes..." he still spoke uncomfortably. "Like my father did."

"No, Billy. I'm not going away. I promise."

"Terry?" Billy spoke a little more firmly.

"Yes?"

"I've never..."

"Never what, Billy?" Terry tried to encourage him.

"I've never talked about my father like this..."

Terry checked his rearview mirror again and could see tears in the boy's eyes. He reached back and touched Billy's arm. They stopped at a red light. Tammy broke a brief silence.

"Terry, do you have any kids?"

"No."

"Why not?"

"Not sure I'd make a good father."

"Sure you would," she coaxed. "It's easy."

"Oh?" he played along, a tinge of humor in his voice. "What would I have to do?"

"Well, take them out for pizza, play ball with them, and listen to music."

"I prob'ly could do that," he chuckled. "If I had kids."

"Well, you just go ahead and have some, Terry," she said bossily. "And we'll show you what to do."

"Sounds like a deal," he laughed.

They got to the house. Terry parked the car and they all went inside.

"So you survived your first outing alone with the kids," Lauren commented.

"Piece of cake," Terry responded.

"They can be challenging."

"Tell me about it."

She smiled. Once again they were sitting on her living room couch. It being a school day tomorrow, the kids had gone to bed early. But not before Terry had spent obligatory time in each of their rooms, listening to music and listening to baseball.

She sneezed. She tried to mask it with a cough. The result was a fairly dismal exhibit of both. He did his best to choke off a laugh.

She was dressed in the same housecoat in which she'd seen them off hours earlier. "Yellowish-green frumpy" would best describe it. Nevertheless, he found both it and her utterly charming. All the more following her sneeze-cough.

"You know," he said, "I was thinking the other day. From the very first time I saw you and the kids back in El Paso my luck changed. I went from being stuck in the minors to making the majors and being here with you. Like you and the kids are my lucky charms."

She didn't reply. Instead, she smiled that alluring smile. Perhaps she didn't speak because if she had, it might have brought on another sneeze.

"Like it was yesterday," he reminisced, "I recall Karen coming up to me that miserable hot day and asking for my autograph for Billy."

She shook her head slightly in acknowledgment. And then she couldn't hold back another sneeze. Plus, the accompanying cough, which this time was much stronger than before. Two more sneezes followed, each more potent than the prior.

"I think I'd better call it a night," she said.

"Me too."

"Baseball tomorrow?"

"Tomorrow night."

She got up from the couch. He didn't move. She looked a little puzzled.

"Forgot to mention," he said, patting the couch, "I'm staying here tonight."

"That's not a good idea."

"Sure it is."

"How do you figure?" she asked.

"Long way to go late at night."

"I'm too weak now to argue," she shrugged. "But what do I tell the kids in the morning?"

"That I stayed over," he quickly answered, "so I could drive them to school."

She shrugged again.

"Any problems at school?" Lauren asked soon after Terry got back from dropping the kids off.

"No. Tammy just wanted me to go to her class with her."

"Really?" she questioned, looking concerned. "Was she afraid to walk by herself?"

"Oh, no," he grinned. "She just wanted to show her classmates a real live baseball player. Not one who was only on TV."

She grinned too. For a change, instead of on the living room couch, they were in her kitchen. She'd made breakfast for the kids before they left, and was making it for the two of them now.

"Been thinking about your proposal," he said following a brief silence between them.

"What proposal?" she asked, although her expression indicated she had a pretty good idea.

"You know...about us getting married."

"That wasn't a proposal," she objected.

"Sure it was," he chuckled. "You said the court would only consider me as a parent if I was married. You're the only one I would marry. Therefore, it's a proposal."

"Your logic leaves a bit to be desired," she smiled.

"What do you expect from a knuckleball pitcher?"

She laughed. She poured hot cereal into two bowls on the kitchen table and they sat down. Juice, toast and coffee were already on the table.

"Anyway," he went on, "why is it so important to the court that I be married?"

"Well, if we were married and you're living with us...with the kids, then adoption is the logical next step. After all, you'd have custody already. What's that old axiom...? Possession is nine-tenths of the law."

"So it's a done deal," he grinned again. "All I have to do is accept your proposal."

"Hey, wait a minute," she raised her hand in protest. "Slow down here. What about your promise?"

"What promise?"

"No sympathy."

"This isn't sympathy."

"What is it then?" she raised her voice a little. "A man doesn't just take on a sick woman *and* her kids."

"It's exactly what a man does when he loves her *and* her kids."

Neither of them spoke again right away. As if to accentuate his last statement, he quickly gulped down his juice, and then took a big bite of toast. Meanwhile, she didn't touch her food.

"What about finances?" she asked.

"We'd manage."

"I've put *some* money away," she said. "And Steven told me he'd help. But the medical bills and children are expensive."

"We'd manage," he repeated. "I'm getting a big league salary now."

"You think it would be easy?" she continued her theme. "Watching me waste away. Possibly having to raise the children all by yourself."

"You're raising them all by yourself."

"And you're willing to finish the job if that's the way things work out?"

"Yes," he replied emphatically. "I would be."

"You'd like to be *the closer*..." she sounded just as emphatic. "That's your role. In baseball *and* in *life.* Am I right?"

He'd never thought of it that way. She sneezed. And coughed. Both hearty ones. So that what he thought at that moment was how cute she looked as she tried to cover her nose and her mouth at the same time with one hand. While wearing the same frumpy housecoat she had on yesterday and last night.

"Try to eat a little and then go back to bed," he suggested.

"What will you do?"

"Go pick up the kids later. Then go to baseball."

"What about till then?"

"Make myself at home," he pointed inside, toward the living room couch.

She offered no dispute. No doubt because if she did, it would only invite more sneezes and coughs

CHAPTER THIRTY

"Sleep?" Terry asked from his usual station on the couch as Lauren entered the room.

"Quite a bit."

"Oh, I checked into a transportation service," he motioned toward some notations on a pad. "They'll take the kids to school or pick them up in a pinch."

"Good resource development, Mr. Closer. Baseball doesn't work out, you could always try counseling."

He laughed. She sat down next to him. She was wearing the same housecoat. He noticed how red her nose was.

"There's food in the fridge for lunch," she offered.

"I know. I made us a couple of sandwiches."

"Making yourself at home," she said, a tinge of accusation in her voice.

"Told you I would. Someone once told me possession is nine-tenths of the law."

She smiled. They got up and went into the kitchen. He took the sandwiches out of the refrigerator and put them on the table. When they sat down, he caught her fighting off another sneeze.

"Hope you like it," he said. "You hardly nibbled at breakfast."

She nibbled now, and then nodded approvingly. He felt relieved when she took a second bite, much bigger than the first. Possibly to encourage her, he took a very large bite of his own sandwich.

"I want you to know something," he spoke soothingly while touching her left elbow.

"Yes?" she gazed at him.

"I admire your strength."

"Strength? What strength? Look at me coughing and sneezing. Sleeping half the day away."

For emphasis, she both sneezed and coughed. He pointed to her sandwich and she took another bite.

"You know what I mean," he said. "If it were me..."

"What did you think I would do?" she interrupted. "Give up! Sit around feeling sorry for myself. I don't have that luxury. Not with the kids."

He nodded. Of course none of this surprised him. Not if he knew her in the least. He pointed to the sandwich again, and she took another bite.

"Speaking of the kids," she sighed. "You know my biggest regret...?"

"What?"

"Maybe...not getting to see them grow up."

She sighed again. He shook his head. He could see tears beginning to form in her eyes. Once more he pointed to the sandwich and she took another nibble.

"Once you finish," he said, "we're going to go into your bedroom and take another nap."

"We?"

"Yes, we," he spoke firmly. "I want to hold you."

There was nothing distinctive about her bed, and certainly nothing fancy. Probably its best feature was its jet-black fluffy down bedspread. The room itself was small and furnished simply. Numerous drawings by the children, at various ages, dotted the white walls.

For sleepwear, Terry borrowed a heavy oversized brown sweatshirt from her. Meanwhile, she stayed with her ubiquitous housecoat. It was she who slipped back the bedspread and blanket, without the slightest ceremony.

"I hope you don't catch my cold," she said as she slid into bed.

"If I have, I already did," he replied, joining her.

"More knuckleball logic?" she laughed.

But he could tell her laughter was tense. And he was far from relaxed himself. No question, neither of them had anticipated the afternoon winding up like this.

She lay on her back. From her left, he put both arms around her. At first he held her loosely, and then he tightened his grip. Her body, slim and lithe, felt good against his as she rolled over on her right side. He nudged even closer.

Seemingly within seconds, she was asleep. It took him much longer; however, he did manage to doze off.

How it happened could probably only be explained by a combination of factors. When they woke, she was obviously drowsy from sleep, from her cold, and from cold medication she was undoubtedly taking. He, on the other hand, regularly felt amorous after sleeping. Plus, when she tried unsuccessfully (her drowsiness was clearly overwhelming) to edge out of bed, her housecoat slid high up her thighs.

Her legs were beautiful. The only other time he noticed them was during their "Saturday night date," when they went dancing. She definitely had dancer's legs—long, slender and femininely athletic. And, after reaching out to touch them in his own drowsy state, he found them to be very soft and malleable.

"I hope you don't catch my cold," she repeated her warning from earlier.

"If I have, I already did," he snickered his same response.

Once her housecoat slid up, it never came back down. And there was only a short flimsy nightgown underneath. She made only a brief attempt to resist, one that seemingly merely heightened their lovemaking.

It took a while for him to move his focus away from her legs, but when he finally did, he found other parts of her no less delightful.

Terry was sitting on the living room couch, putting on his shoes, about to leave to go pick up the kids, when Lauren surprised him by coming out of her bedroom fully dressed. They'd already agreed that he'd pick them up by himself. In fact, when he'd left the bedroom half an hour ago, she was just beginning another nap.

"What are you doing?" he asked.

"I'm going with you."

"There's no reason," he disagreed.

"There's one *big* reason," she said firmly. "I want to be with you."

CHAPTER THIRTY-ONE

Terry picked up the ball in the center of the diamond and began his warm-ups. He was already perspiring heavily. He glanced toward the facade below the top deck of the stadium, at the digital thermometer there. Ninety-five degrees. Ninety-five degrees at ten o'clock at night! Where else could this be but Texas?

It was the start of the bottom of the ninth in the final game of their final road trip of the season. Things had gone well in the first five games. Two out of three in Chicago, and a split of the first two here. Terry had recorded saves in the Chicago wins, but had yet to appear here.

They still trailed Texas by four and a half in the division. A win tonight, though, would boost them into a tie for the wild card, since New York had lost earlier that evening. All Terry had to do was protect a 7-4 lead.

Seven-four. Wasn't that the exact score when he'd entered that first game of the season, on Easter Sunday right here in Texas? When he'd blown an easy save, surrendering a grand slam in the ninth inning. That was in the minor leagues, however. And in El Paso, not Dallas where they now were.

Yet the memory was strong. The oppressive heat. Pitching Coach Collum's negativity. His own anger and disappointment over not making the majors. The anxiety regarding whether he'd soon lose his job. And, finally, the humiliating loss.

The first Texas batter rudely brought him back to the present, lining his first pitch to center for a single. The next hitter walked on a close 3-2 pitch. The following batter grounded a two hopper to shortstop Oates, a perfect double play ball. Except he booted it. The bases were loaded.

Wasn't this exactly the way that opening game in El Paso had gone? With the next hitter slugging the grand slam. Would the script be identical? Or could he somehow alter it?

Rick came out of the Oakland dugout. For an instant Terry mistook him for Collum. Was the heat playing tricks? As Rick reached the mound, Terry shook his head vigorously, trying to clear it.

"You okay?" Rick asked.

"Like a bad dream," Terry muttered, more to himself than to Rick.

"Better wake up."

Once Rick left to return to the dugout, Terry shook his head again. This was no dream, it was very much reality. It was a definite test. His test—bases loaded, no outs, Texas—the heat.

He felt as if he was dealing with both the present and the past. With so much at stake. For him. And for the team. He couldn't blow this save. Blow their chance to tie New York in the wild card race.

He walked off the mound, toward second base. Briefly, he thought about Lauren. About how he'd phoned her at least once a day while he'd been away. About all she'd been through. About how much he loved her.

Then his mind switched back to Texas. In particular to that awful first month of the season in El Paso. How hopeless he'd felt. How he'd come so close to quitting.

That seemed so long ago. With so much happening since. Was he actually the same person? As he'd told Lauren, he was going nowhere then. Stuck in El Paso. Yet, soon after Karen had asked for his autograph, he'd managed to change the direction of his life. If he could do that, maybe he could change the direction of this game. Alter its script.

He stepped back on the mound. He glanced again at the digital thermometer. Still ninety-five. After removing his cap, he wiped his forehead with his arm. Then gazed at Bailey for the sign. Fastball. No, not a fastball. Hadn't that been what the batter back in El Paso had hit for the grand slam?

170

He rubbed his glove along his belt, shaking off the sign. What was wrong with the diver? But Bailey seemed adamant, flashing fastball again.

Terry reluctantly gave in. Maybe it was a good idea, especially if the hitter was looking for a knuckler. Plus, he didn't have to throw the fastball for a strike. At the last second, though, he decided to try to throw it for a strike. And threw a perfect one, over the outside corner at the knees. The batter, fooled, reached for the pitch and tapped another grounder to shortstop, this one to Oates's left. This time Oates fielded it and, without breaking stride, stepped on second base and threw to first. Double play. A runner did score, making it 7-5, but now there were two outs.

Terry began the next batter with the diver. He swung, lifting a little pop fly behind the mound. Terry quickly scanned the infielders racing toward the ball, and saw none of them would get it before it fell. Billy's catch, ending the game the night of his no hitter, flashed through his mind. Hurrying back toward the ball, Terry reached up over his head and behind himself, and snagged the ball in the webbing of his glove. Exactly as Billy had done.

The game was over. He had gotten the final three outs on just two pitches. He had survived Texas. He had survived the heat. He had passed the test. In celebration, he tossed the ball high into the air.

With only nine games left on the schedule, Oakland had tied New York for the wild card.

"Another attack," Lauren's voice sounded very weak and distant over the phone.

"Oh, no!" he gasped into his bungalow phone. "Where are you?"

"Hospital."

"Which one?" he stammered, becoming more and more alarmed.

"Near the house."

"I'm on my way."

He scrambled around the room, trying to get dressed. He was groggy himself, her early morning call ending a night's sleep already abbreviated by a 3:00 a.m. arrival home from the road trip. He had many more questions to ask her, but at least he was thinking clearly enough not to ask them during the phone call, as weak as she sounded.

Moments later, he rushed out the door.

It took Terry much longer to reach her than he'd hoped. The morning rush hour traffic crossing the bridge into San Francisco was very heavy. Although he had no problem locating the hospital (he'd driven by it several times while taking the kids to or from school), he did have trouble finding her room because the hospital was so spread out, with a couple of areas under construction.

When he finally did get to her, he was even more alarmed than earlier. Asleep, she looked pale and lifeless, much like Carly after her overdose. He sat down in a chair next to her bed. Eventually, she opened her eyes and smiled faintly at him.

"Feeling okay?" he began with the questions he would like to have asked during their phone conversation.

"Not so good."

"The attack? Was it bad?"

"Bad. The worst one yet."

"When did it happen?" he probed on, since she seemed to be getting more alert.

"Middle of the night."

"Why didn't you call me?"

"I tried. You must have been flying. So I called my brother."

"Oh."

"He lives close. Came right over and got me to emergency."

"Are you in danger now?"

"No. No longer."

"The kids okay?" he altered direction a little.

"Steven took them to school."

He nodded. He detected hoarseness in her voice, as if talking was becoming difficult. So he gave her a break. He noticed she had on a white robe, obviously furnished by the hospital. For some reason, he thought about her yellowish-green housecoat, and considered offering to go get it and bring it here.

"Baseball today?" she interrupted his thoughts with her own question.

"No. Not until tomorrow night."

"Want to pick up the kids from school?"

"Sure."

"And stay in the house tonight?"

"Sure."

"Use my bed."

"I can sleep in the living room on the couch."

"No. I insist. Use my bed."

He didn't argue. Really, she'd probably never find out where he'd slept anyway. He considered asking her when she might be released from the hospital, but she closed her eyes. She was soon asleep again.

He watched her and observed how peaceful she looked. Eventually, a female orderly entered the room. He got up from the chair, kissed Lauren on the cheek, and went out into the hallway.

Terry had no further luck whatsoever conversing with Lauren before he had to leave to pick up the children. All she did was sleep. Most of the time he simply sat there, watching her. She hardly even stirred, except for the two or three occasions that he kissed her cheek again, whenever he left the room.

He stopped at the nurses' station once to try and find out more about her condition. When she might be released. The head nurse, a very short woman whose right arm was in a sling, was completely noncommittal. Especially since he wasn't a family member. And her grave expression certainly didn't provide him any optimism.

On his way to the school, her brother came to mind. Certainly he, being a doctor, would give him some solid information.

"Doesn't look like your mama will be home tonight," Terry told the three kids.

"We know," Karen said glumly. "Uncle Steven told us."

Terry nodded. They had put in their order at a pizza parlor, and had just sat down at a table. Under the circumstances, Terry didn't have the heart to deny

Tammy's usual request. Especially, he pondered while grinning inwardly, if it meant she might offer him some "much needed" parenting advice.

"What about some video games while we wait for our pizza?" he suggested.

"Oh, no," Karen stated. "Mama always makes us do our homework before we play."

"Okay...you know she wants me to stay with you tonight."

"All night?" Tammy bubbled.

"So I can take you to school tomorrow morning..."

"Can you help me with my homework like Mommy does?" she pretty well ignored his explanation.

"I can try."

"Mine too?" Billy asked.

"What about mine?" Karen of course required equal treatment.

"I don't know," Terry chuckled. "Tammy's kindergarten might be the limit of my ability."

Terry did reach Steven late that afternoon. He was almost as noncommittal as the head nurse had been. Yes, she'd had by far her worst attack. And the others had been pretty bad. How long would she remain in the hospital? Possibly for a while, if for no other reason than for close observation.

"What about the kids?" Terry asked.

"Lauren said you might stay overnight whenever you can."

"I will."

"Otherwise they can stay with me. But I usually work late."

"We're home for the rest of our schedule," Terry volunteered. "They can go to the games and sit in the players' wives and families' section."

"Good," Steven said.

And then Steven excused himself to go back to work.

Getting into bed that night, Terry felt very strange. Certainly not because her bed had any unusual characteristics, since it didn't. And certainly not because he wasn't sleeping in his own bed in the bungalow. After all, with so many hotel rooms populating his lengthy baseball history, he'd probably slept in over a thousand assorted beds.

No, his discomfort had much more to do with Lauren herself. The fact that he was in love with her. The fact that the two of them had slept in this bed together, if only once and very briefly, and he missed her.

Much earlier, he'd taken the kids to see her. With pretty much the same result of his earlier visit, since she was so tired. Following a few hugs, kisses and tears, they spent most of the time simply watching her sleep. They ended up not staying terribly long.

Lying there now, tossing and turning, he did achieve a smile when he recalled what happened before the hospital. The "homework venture." Fortunately, kindergarten *was* within his grasp. And he avoided any verdict regarding higher grades by begging off to reheat the pizza they hadn't eaten at the parlor.

For probably an hour, he remained in Lauren's bed, continuing to toss and turn. Finally, when it became apparent he wasn't about to fall asleep, he got up and went into the living room. He lay down on the couch, where he and Lauren had sat so many times.

Almost instantly, he fell asleep.

CHAPTER THIRTY-TWO

"How's Carly and Joshua?" Terry asked Murdoch over the phone, after dropping off the children at school.

"Come over and see for yourself."

"Can I bring some company?"

"Definitely," Murdoch answered buoyantly.

"The kids wear you out?" Lauren asked.

"We did fine," Terry replied.

"Tammy get her pizza?"

"How'd you know?"

"Not exactly rocket science," she smiled.

He smiled back. He was happy with the way she looked this morning. Still very pale, but certainly much better than yesterday and last night, and she seemed much more alert.

"What about later?" she asked.

"Later?"

"For the kids."

"I'll take them to our game," he informed her. "Some of the players' wives will keep an eye on them."

She nodded. He considered telling her about his conversation with Steven. That between the two of them, they could manage. A nurse came in the room then, though.

"I can't blame you if you're scared," she said the instant the nurse left, while sitting up a little in bed.

"Scared? About what?"

"About the kids. About me. About all this stuff." For emphasis, she extended the palm of her hand out toward the hospital room.

"I'm not scared," he insisted.

Actually he *had* become a little scared this morning. The responsibility. The newness (promptly reinforced by his having to oversee three youngsters getting ready for

176

school). And of course her condition. But he wasn't about to admit to any of it. Especially with her showing such improvement.

"I can't blame you if you turn it down," she spoke seriously.

"Turn what down?"

"My proposal."

"What proposal?" he asked.

"The one you keep accusing me of making," she grinned.

Finally, he caught on that she was referring to the subject of marriage. Possibly his dullness could be attributed to all that had happened lately. All that was happening now.

"When?" was all he could muster.

"Might be a good idea to move quickly. These attacks...they keep coming."

"When?" he repeated, more eagerly.

"I don't want to interfere with baseball in any way. I thought at the end of your season, but I'm not so sure we should wait."

"We have an off day Monday," he said even more eagerly.

"Monday," she began counting on her fingers. "Three days. Should give me enough time for the arrangements. Ever been married in a hospital?"

"Hospital!" he exclaimed. "You mean the wedding'll be here."

"Already got permission from management. They're okay with it as long as I stay in bed."

"Wow!" he managed.

"I've already started preparations."

"You're amazing," he uttered. "Flat on your back..."

"Steven said he'd help."

"What can *I* do?"

"What you're doing. Looking after the kids. Just make sure all of you are here."

He nodded and smiled.

"Promise me something," she went on.

"Sure."

"Promise me that none of this—the wedding, me, the kids—that none of this interferes with baseball in any way."

"I promise."

"Tell me."

"I promise," he raised his right hand mockingly, as though he was reciting an oath. "I promise that none of this will interfere with baseball."

"Oh...and Terry," she added as apparent afterthought. "Wear that nice coat and tie to the wedding. The one you wore on our Saturday night date."

He smiled again.

The "company" Terry referred to during his phone conversation with Murdoch was of course Billy, Karen and Tammy. The visit to Murdoch's apartment had gone well so far. As at Carly's drug program graduation, the kids were transfixed by tiny Joshua. In fact, they had spent nearly the entire hour of the visit playing on the floor with him, and with Carly.

"Well, kids, time for us to leave," Terry said while getting up off the living room couch.

"They could stay here with Joshua and me, Uncle Terry," Carly offered. "While you and Dad go to your game. There's plenty of food in the fridge."

He looked at the children, still on the floor. All three nodded, indicating preference to stay. He headed for the door. Carly joined him there.

"Lauren called earlier, Uncle Terry. Dad's taking Joshua and me to visit her tomorrow."

"Nice."

"She going to be okay?"

"She's much better today."

"She told me about your plans. Congratulations."

"Goes for me too," Murdoch echoed her sentiment.

"The kids..." Terry said softly to Carly. "You seem to like them."

"Of course I do. They're Lauren's."

"I'll be here to pick them up right after the game."

"Uncle Terry, if you or Lauren ever need help with them..."

178

"Thanks."

"Goes for me too," Murdoch seconded.

ALAN MINDELL

Chapter Thirty-Three

Terry was amazed at how smoothly the wedding went.
As if plans had been underway for months instead of
merely a few days, every detail was meticulously attended
to. All he had to do, as Lauren had insisted, was show up
with the children. And of course wear the same brown
coat and tie he'd worn for their only "real date" in their
nearly six month history.

The hospital room was decorated remarkably, with
flowers, trees and shrubbery. Almost as though the
ceremony was taking place outside, in a lovely garden.
Lauren's bed fit the decor, with bedspread and pillowcases
in elaborate floral design.

Steven conducted the wedding. As a doctor, he'd gotten
special permission from appropriate officials. Murdoch
was Terry's best man. Rick was the father figure who
presented the bride, although in this case all he did was
stand beside her, since she never left the bed.

Carly, Karen and Tammy served as bridesmaids. They
had helped Lauren into a beautiful white gown before the
other participants arrived. Little Joshua, ably assisted by
Billy, performed as ring bearer.

Once Steven pronounced Terry and Lauren husband
and wife, Terry bent over the bed and kissed his new bride.
All the others applauded.

"Kiss Mommy again," Tammy grinned at Terry once
everyone except his new family had gone.

"Oh, you like that," he replied, also grinning.

"So does Mommy."

"How do you know?"

"She told us."

Lauren—back in hospital clothing—looking weary by
then, also looked embarrassed. Unable to tell how she felt
about Tammy's request, he chose the safe response of

kissing her forehead. When she didn't resist, he put his arms around her and kissed her lips. Predictably, led by Tammy, the children applauded.

"Now," Lauren said, still looking embarrassed, "time for all of you to leave."

The children groaned.

"School tomorrow," she chided.

Another groan.

"Have you done your homework?"

That got a different reaction. The children walked to the door, Terry following. But he paused, then went back to his new wife to say good bye. At the bed, he observed that her eyes were closed and her breathing was deep. No question, she was asleep already.

He touched her hand briefly, and then headed for the door again.

Much later, after the children had been in bed for quite a while, Terry went into their rooms and checked them. They were all asleep. Then he slipped out of the house and returned to the hospital. No way should Lauren be alone her entire wedding night, without at least a visit from her new husband.

He found her as he'd left her—asleep. He held her hand. Twice he kissed her forehead. He even lay on top of the bed with her, briefly. She stirred several times, but didn't wake.

He remained perhaps two hours before returning home. After getting there, he promptly checked the children again. They were still asleep.

Terry didn't even try Lauren's bed that night. It almost seemed unfaithful to sleep in his bride's bed on their wedding night, with her not there. Instead, he went to the living room couch.

He didn't have much luck falling asleep there either. The wedding repeatedly flashed through his mind. He kept seeing Lauren in her beautiful white gown, confined to bed, looking very frail. It didn't seem fair. A young woman, with what should have been a whole new life ahead, possibly so close to the end.

He tried to focus on being more positive. Maybe she'd soon get over this particular bout and come home. Maybe once she got here and they could start living together, she'd find new energy to begin a full recovery.

It was certainly something to hope for.

CHAPTER THIRTY-FOUR

It was the top of the seventh. Final scheduled game of the season, against Detroit. Oakland led 6-0, on a pair of Murdoch three-run homers. A win clinched the wild card, despite New York's victory earlier this afternoon. Opening game of the playoffs would be in Cleveland, in two days.

Terry sat in the left field bullpen, by himself at one end of the bench. Earlier, it had crossed his mind several times that maybe he shouldn't be here, at the stadium. Not this soon anyhow. Not with the memorial service for Lauren just last evening. But then, hadn't Lauren made it clear that she didn't want to interfere with baseball in any way?

He gazed up into the grandstand behind him, toward where the players' wives, families and guests sat. This being Sunday, no school, Billy, Karen and Tammy were there. Sitting with Carly and Joshua.

Terry glanced at Murdoch nearby, in left field. Murdoch had attended the memorial service with Carly and Joshua. Afterward, he had pulled Terry aside and emphasized that he and Carly were serious about helping him with the children.

Terry looked up at the kids again. Although he knew they were sad, he thought he saw Tammy smile at him. Carly too. He wondered whether Murdoch would ever tell Carly that he, Terry, wasn't her real uncle. Or whether he already had told her. Not that it mattered. What mattered was she had obviously altered her life, and was clearly an entirely different person than the one he'd first met that night in Hollywood.

He turned toward the third base dugout and barely managed to spot Rick in one corner. He'd also attended the service, and had given Terry a hug both before and after. The first time they'd ever exchanged any significant physical affection. Causing Terry to flash back to his own father. In many ways, hadn't Rick assumed that role?

Other memories remained from the service. His own incredible sorrow, which had been constant ever since Lauren's passing. All three kids breaking down. And his own response to it—that despite their reaction, he knew Lauren had prepared them well for this day.

Yes, as he sat there on the bullpen bench, these memories were strong. But there was a memory that was much more vivid than any from the service. He and Lauren were in her hospital room alone at about 3 a.m. on her last night. He was holding her hand while she slept, when she took her final labored breath. A moment he knew would always be with him.

Afterward, numb, he'd returned to the sleeping children. Once more now, he glanced up at them in the grandstand. This time he thought all three smiled back.

His gaze returned to the field. To the splendidly manicured grass. Surrounded by the colossal stadium outlined in green and gold. Everything looked just the same as that first time, about five months ago, when he first came to the majors.

Five months? Was that all the time that had passed? It seemed more like five years.

Much earlier today, long before the game began, Rick had approached him. He informed him that he wouldn't be calling on him to pitch this afternoon. Out of respect for Lauren. Terry disagreed, and had adamantly conveyed his feelings to Rick.

Now, as he sat in the bullpen, any lingering doubts about his being here, at the stadium, were gone. He *would* pitch today if he was needed. That's what Lauren would have wanted, that's what she had made him promise to do.

After all, he was *the closer.*

The End